11/08

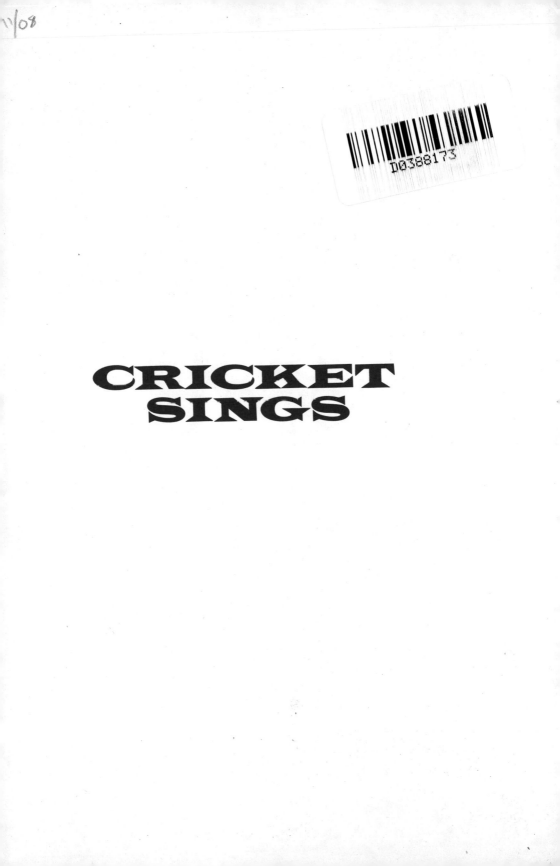

CRICKET SINGS

D0388173

CRICKET SINGS

A NOVEL OF PRE-COLUMBIAN CAHOKIA

KATHLEEN KING

OHIO UNIVERSITY PRESS

ATHENS, OHIO

©Copyright 1983 by Kathleen King
Printed in the United States of America.
All rights reserved.

Library of Congress Cataloging in Publication Data

King, Kathleen, 1948
Cricket sings.

1. Mississippian culture—Fiction.   2.   Indians
of North America—Illinois—Fiction.   I.   Title.
PS3561.I4797C7   1983   813'.54   82-8046
ISBN 0-8214-0704-X   AACR2
ISBN 0-8214-0705-8 pbk.

12   11   10   09   08   07   06   05   04   9 8 7 6 5 4

FIC
KING

Contents

Introduction

Located near the confluence of the Mississippi and Missouri rivers, the Cahokia site has been occupied since at least 700 A.D. By 900 A.D. the settlement had become distinctly "Mississippian," the center of a culture characterized by cities built around ceremonial earth mounds. Archaeologists estimate that the city covered six square miles and had a population of up to 40,000.

The highly organized Mississippian culture utilized city planning, class structure, accurate astronomy, and a far-flung trade network. A stockade-like log wall encircled the central 400 acres of the city. At least 100 earth mounds were built in this area. Monks Mound, the "Holy Hill" of *Cricket Sings,* is the largest earth mound in North America: 100 feet high with a base area of more than 14 acres. All the dirt which composes these mounds was carried from borrow pits in baskets on the backs of workers. Some mounds were ceremonial in nature, while others were the dwelling places of the upper classes. Rectangular mounds often held charnel houses where the bodies of the dead decayed until they were suitable for burial in nearby conical mounds.

No one is certain what happened to the Mississippian people. Archaeologists speculate that the need for wood, both for the stockade, which was rebuilt four times, and for cooking and heating, resulted in depletion of the environment. A concurrent climate shift may have altered growing conditions. Disease is also a possibility. No evidence has been found to indicate that these people were overrun by invaders, despite their extensive fortifications.

To my knowledge, this book is the first attempt to combine the archaeological facts about Cahokia with a story. The culture of the People is based both on direct research related to Cahokia and studies of historic Amerindians. Many tribes believed in windigos, mystical cannibals, and some experienced a "windigo psychosis," in which the entire tribe became convinced they were turning into cannibals. Psychedelic drugs were commonly used during religious ceremonies. My selection of Datura, or jimson weed, as a major psychedelic used by the People is based on William Chmurny's report that a seed of this plant was found during an archaeological dig at Cahokia.

I owe thanks to many people: to my son for the many evenings he spent playing chess while I was at the typewriter; to the archaeologists and anthropologists whose research was so useful; and finally to Jacqueline Jackson, whose help and encouragement were greatly appreciated.

Kathleen King
Williamsville, Illinois
June 28, 1980

Prologue: Shadows

Sun is pulling his soft blanket of Night over the City. Half a day's walk in every direction from the Central Plaza the People are adding wood to their fires, gathering around this bit of Sun allotted to them.

About the bases of the great mounds which dot the City the air is darker, damp with the scent of crushed grass. Many have come to the City to share in this time of Celebration and the usual paths are widening to accommodate them. From the Great Water to the North and the Water of Tears in the South the People have come home.

On the Holiest Hill the Priests begin Ceremonies, their hearts timed to the drums which shape their lives. Here, higher than many men standing upon each other's shoulders, the Priests wait for the sleeper to wake.

Among peaked-roof thatched houses the families of Honored and Warriors gather to gossip, copper bracelets jingling, shell necklaces clattering. Slender youths play the flute for their lovers, mournful songs hanging over the City like ghosts. The Ordinaries rest, their backs twisted from a lifetime of hauling baskets of dirt to build the mounds ever higher.

Grandmothers and grandfathers light fires for their families. Old ones are precious knowledge to the People. Stories are told, and in the flames the Gods dance. Children listen and remember.

CHAPTER ONE
Beginnings

The night was cold and Cricket Sings stooped at the woodpile looking for a hunk of dried maple. In the dusk her old, short-sighted eyes squinted, drawing wrinkles across her cheeks. She selected a piece of wood and dragged the small trunk toward the rim of firelight, scarring the bark as it scratched over rocks on the ground. Ceremonially, Cricket Sings walked to the fire and dropped the large end of the log onto the coals. A shower of sparks erupted toward the stars. She turned her face up, following the sparks, then hobbled to a place on the smokeless side of the fire.

"I am very old," she said, "and it is time to tell my stories."

The brown faces of the People gathered around the fire reflected the glow of the flames, as well as their excitement at once more sharing the history of their kind. Cricket Sings began.

"Before the World there was only Night, but the darkness cracked and a light peered out. It was the Sun and together Sun and Night pulled until they made a place between them for the World. Sun was lonely, so he took a little darkness from Night and mixed it with his own light to create Moon. She was the first woman.

"Together Sun and Moon made the World. They molded light and darkness from their bodies to make the earth. Sun and Moon made the plants and animals as we make pots from clay, each one a little different. The Gods baked their creations in the heat of Sun, then gave each thing a spirit and name to fit its nature. The World was begun.

"At first the Gods were pleased with their new creation, but gradually Sun's disappointment grew. The World was not alive, instead waiting patiently and changing only where the Gods touched. Sun wanted the World to surprise him. He brooded for a long time, then asked Moon for her opinion on the matter. Sensible Moon suggested making love because many fine decisions grow out of the talk between husband and wife after this most pleasurable activity. So Sun and Moon worshipped together and it was more beautiful than ever before. The rhythmic surges of their great bodies created Wind. At the end fierce sparks flew, becoming Lightning. Those sparks which rose too high and got stuck in Night are now called stars. When Sun and Moon rested, they saw that already the actions of Lightning and Wind had begun to change the World. As Sun proclaimed the new ones Young Gods, Moon's joyous laughter rippled out, creating the sisters Clouds and Rain.

"The World was very good, but the Gods wanted to talk with other creatures. There was much discussion of how these new beings should look. As Sun watched the World, he saw a huge oak tree in full leaf near a great river. He thought about the strength and long life of oak. Sun called Lightning to him and pointed to the tree.

'Go strike that tree into two halves for me.'

"Lightning nodded and flew to do his creator's bidding. The tree was split into equal halves and at the same instant the Sun gave life to each half. So the People began, each man or woman one half of that great tree, the oak.

"The Gods watched the World change each day. Sun liked to see his light play across the prairie and forest. The Gods marveled at the tiny living beasts they had made as the People began to roam the World. We are here and it is good. Now I am finished talking and you young ones may go to bed so an old woman can sit by the fire in peace."

Cricket Sings nodded to her daughter, Doe Eyes, who smiled in reply. "Please, mother, just one more story?" the young woman asked. "Tell us how Beaver got his house!"

Cricket Sings wrinkled her face at her only child, who knew how much the old woman liked stories about Beaver, then turned back to her friends and family, who waited with open faces.

"You know that Sun taught each animal how to build a house suitable for its needs. Well, Beaver built the first house. Sun looked at Beaver and saw sharp teeth, then looked down and saw the webbed feet. Finally Beaver turned around and showed Sun his long, flat tail.

" 'We will find you a home where that tail can be of some use,' said Sun, admiring the handsome appendage. 'Come back in the morning.'

"So Beaver hurried away to find fresh saplings to eat. He was very hungry after waiting for so long and the bark was especially tasty. Beaver ate his fill and then lay down to sleep. Night came with a cold wind. Beaver shivered. He did not like to sleep on the ground. 'I hope Sun finds me a safe, warm home,' Beaver muttered under his breath so the God would not hear. Night was very long and Beaver was afraid when he heard the wolves howling. Animals with sharp teeth get hungry and Beaver was afraid they would eat him.

"Morning was a relief after such a restless Night. Beaver was cold and his muscles had cramped. He shook himself all over and then ate a few tender buds before walking stiffly toward the place where he was to meet Sun. He saw the brilliance of the God ahead and called out. 'Halloo, there, Sun. I am here as you said.'

" 'You are just in time. I have found the perfect home for you, Beaver.'

"Following Sun's voice, Beaver approached the God and found him standing next to a backwater of the river. There were large trees between new young trees and brush all around the water. When Beaver reached the shore he saw that there was only a narrow opening into the main part of the river. He accidentally stepped in the mud with his clean paws and shook first one, then the others. The mud was cold.

"The Sun turned to Beaver. His face was bright and Beaver had to squint.

" 'Hello, my little friend,' said Sun with a smile. 'I have found the perfect home for you.' As he said this, the God lifted his arm toward the water in a wide sweep.

" 'Ah, ah, it's pretty wet out there, Sun, perhaps some higher ground would be better for a Beaver.'

"Sun scowled, but then smiled as he realized that Beaver did not yet understand the use of his lovely teeth, feet, and tail. 'Come here,' he said, taking Beaver by the arm and dragging him to the edge of the water. 'Look at your teeth. See how long and sharp and yellow they are? Tell me, Beaver, what do you do with those teeth?'

"Beaver peered cautiously at his reflection, careful to keep his toes out of the mud. 'I gnaw little branches and eat the tender buds,' was his reply. 'They are my favorite.'

" 'That's exactly right, Beaver. You are very thoughtful and have strong teeth besides, which will enable you to cut down whole trees. You will have a snug and sturdy house made of wood.'

"Beaver's eyes grew wide. He blinked and looked back over his shoulder at the trees. 'Those are very *BIG* trees, Sun.'

"Sun threw back his head and laughed at the lazy Beaver, then pointed to Beaver's feet. 'Look at your paws.'

"Beaver, glad that he had been noticed as a thinker, picked up first one front paw and then the other. He looked carefully at each. The toes were long, with webs stretched between. He shook his head, then turned with much difficulty so that he faced in the wrong direction entirely, picking up first one rear foot and then the second. Shaking off a piece of mud, Beaver considered the rearness of these feet. 'They greatly resemble my two feet in the front, but larger,' he said. With a grunt, Beaver turned back around to the front. 'Well, what does all this mean?' He looked up at the God.

"Sun laughed and pointed to the water. 'You will make a good swimmer with those webbed paws.'

"Beaver's face wrinkled. He reached out one paw to the water, but jerked it back. The mud had not been nearly as cold as the water. He shook his paw very hard. 'See here, Sun, I don't mind getting my feet wet, but couldn't we wait for summer?'

'Beaver, all of you will get wet. You will swim out to your new house in the middle of this pond!'

"Beaver was shocked into silence and turned away. Why would Sun suggest something so unsuited to his nature?

" 'Beaver,' Sun was tapping him on the shoulder. 'Friend, turn around here.'

"Reluctantly, Beaver turned around until once again he faced the water. His big tail lay across his feet. 'I will do it, Sun, but only because you are a God.'

"Beaver began to make his house. He liked gnawing down the trees, making each piece even and useful, finding just the right place for the logs. He built a platform of branches in the middle of the pond, then started work on a fine domed house. He made a door to face the east, where he and Sun had stood looking out on the river. After all this work Beaver grew tired. All he wanted to do was crawl into his house and flop down on the floor. But something was wrong; he was cold, shivering even inside the new house. Then Beaver understood, He had carried water into the house on the outer hairs of his thick fur coat.

"Beaver was so tired he could hardly walk, but he knew he would not be able to sleep until the floor dried, so he went outside and considered how to make the door water tight. There was a big trout living in the branches at the base of the platform. The fish did not move and stared at Beaver with solemn eyes. Coming up into the air with a little choke, the wise Beaver realized that he could make the door underwater and then it could be very narrow. A clever Beaver could swim right into the hole and pull himself out at the top. The narrow opening would squeeze the water from his fur. So Beaver made his new door.

"When it was almost spring Beaver found a wife. Her name was Round Ears and she was very pretty. He liked to walk beside her on the shore. Her chubby body swayed as she chewed and he imitated her with a little dance. They were very happy and when the cubs came Beaver brought his mate the tenderest buds from the slender willows which grew at the end of the pond.

"Far upstream it rained very hard. The winter had been harsh and much snow was melting. The water poured into the river, which began to simmer and turned brown. The angry water raced along the stream and came into the pond through the narrow opening while Beaver and Round Ears were on shore gathering small leaves for their cubs to eat. The water ran into the beaver house and rose over the little ones. Beaver felt the water on his feet and turned to see that the pond had become a lake. Only the topmost branches of the house were dry. Round Ears had moved away around the curve of the shore and Beaver called to her, but a beaver's voice is very soft and she did not hear. He jumped up and down and waved, but her back was turned. Beaver could wait no longer. He jumped into the water and his large flat tail, which he had found useful for steering when swimming, made a loud slapping sound on the water. Beaver heard the noise and out of the corner of his eye saw Round Ears turn toward him in surprise. He picked up his tail and slapped it down hard once more, hearing a splash as his mate jumped into the water. They both raced toward their house.

"It was too late. The inside of the house was full of water and the beloved new ones were limp and dead. Together the parents mourned, and then Beaver sat down to think. He sat in the mud and thought for a whole day. Round Ears came and sat beside him. When the female realized that he was thinking, she sat up straight beside him and together they made a picture. The pond was wide, but the place where water came in was narrow. If they could put something across that place, the water would come in more slowly, and perhaps not get so deep. 'But then the stream would be held back on our side of the dam,' Beaver said out loud.

" 'Yes, but we will build the house higher,' answered Round Ears.

" 'And we can make the dam just like the house. . .'

" 'Out of sticks!'

"The two began to gnaw down small saplings which grew all along the shore. When there was a sizeable pile, Round Ears began to haul the sticks across the pond to the opening. She placed some in the mud at the shore, then went to relieve her mate of the gnawing so he could help with the dam. With two beavers working, they were able to build a good tight dam which kept out the river and held back the stream. A nice deep pond grew and there Round Eyes and Beaver taught the new little ones, born the next spring, to swim. And never again did Beaver shiver and listen to wolves all night in the woods. He was snug and safe in his house and could not even hear the wolves howl."

In the silence at the end of the story, Doe Eyes stood and picked up her sleeping daughter from a robe on the ground. Wolf Hunter followed his wife, carrying their firstborn son in his cradleboard. The baby murmured drowsily in response to the familiar motion. At the door of the house, the young couple turned and bowed to Cricket Sings, who bent her head toward them. She would follow after the fire had burned to coals.

Other women were rising quietly and taking their families home. Running Water waved goodbye to her older sister, then hurried to catch up to her daughters, who were walking toward their home near the palisade. In a few sighs of Wind, Cricket Sings sat alone. She shoved the last stub of her maple log into the fire with a moccasined toe. Sparks flew, reminding the old woman of the lovemaking of Sun and Moon. She smiled. Many a husband would try to equal Sun tonight.

Soon even the dogs were asleep. Cricket Sings stared into the fire, lost in the dance of the flames. She thought of her friend Remember the Fish, the old man who had died that morning, the last of his line. Many times he had given food to her fatherless child, asking nothing in return. Now his body was lying in the charnel house. She shook her head slowly from side to side.

Suddenly, a twig snapped behind the woodpile and the old woman sat frozen by this unusual sound. Her ears strained for other sounds which might reveal what was lurking just beyond the fire's circle of light. There were none. Cricket Sings started at the touch of a hand on her shoulder and turned to see her cousin Yellow Dog, who flattened his hand over her mouth with a "Shh" to stop her frightened cry. She drew a deep breath as he took his hand away.

"What are you doing here, old man?" she whispered. "I thought you were living with your Northern wife's people."

"Be quiet, woman, I have come to enjoy the Celebration of the Sun with my family. My wife's sister married Basket Maker, the one who lives on the far side of the Big Lake. We are camped next to his house. My youngest son, Wounded Deer, has a sickness in his belly and I have come to ask you to make medicine for him."

"This belly sickness, how long has he been hurting?"

"On the trail south yesterday Wounded Deer cried and asked his mother to carry him. Tonight he lies on his side moaning and will not straighten his legs. He is very hot to the touch."

Cricket Sings sighed and gestured toward the door. "Inside is my medicine bag. Get it and we will go to Wounded Deer, but move quietly so that you do not disturb my child and her family."

Yellow Dog rose from his squatting position and walked six paces to the door of the house. Pushing aside the skin covering the doorway, he felt inside for the doeskin bag which contained

Cricket Sings' most precious secrets, slid the bag carefully to the door, then found the long strap and stretched it over his shoulder. He stood and turned to the old woman sitting by the fire.

"Are you ready now?" he asked in an impatient voice.

Cricket Sings rose with a low moan for that creaking in her bones which no medicine could mend. She shook first her good leg, then the other. "Yes, I am ready."

The two cousins set out on the path which ran past the house. The herb woman lived on the sunset side of Big Lake, near the burial mound of her Honored ancestors. The home of Basket Maker was closer to the southern edge of the city, where the corn fields began. The night was quiet, not even the persistent insects hummed. Bright over the lake, a rising full moon outlined the peaked grass houses of the People.

"How are things in the North City, is the trading good?" the old woman questioned.

"The trading is quite good. They mine copper every day now, and of course the People of the City like shining ornaments."

Cricket Sings began again after a pause. "I have heard bad things about the Northerners. It has been said that they eat men as one would eat a deer or rabbit."

"We all have heard stories about the Northern People, but I have never seen them eat men. Our own Priests make sacrifices to the Sun, but of course that is considered a sacred meal."

She did not reply. Sometimes Ordinaries disappeared into the compound on top of the Sun's Holy Hill, but no one ever asked where they had gone. No Honored Men or Warriors had been sacrificed since the death of Magnificent Sun King.

"Your Northern wife, she does not miss her own people on your journeys?"

"The company of her sister is most welcome. My wife is a fine woman, although she does not know how to grow corn. Her own people are from the far North, where there is much copper and they trade for corn and hunt the deer and bear."

"Ahead, is that the Basket Maker's house? He has built a summer kitchen, I see, and hung it with mats. Perhaps some mats would cover my door and windows." The old woman knew that Yellow Dog would deliver freshly woven mats to her doorstep. They would do much to keep the flies off her face in the early morning.

A small fire was burning outside the house. Three children, bundled in robes, slept before the fire. A low, keening sound issued from the house.

"My wife and her sister," Yellow Dog explained. "They fear the boy will die."

Cricket Sings, too, was afraid for the child's life. Evil in the belly was often beyond her medicine, as well as that of the Sun. She saw the false cheer of the flag left from the Sun Priest's earlier visit. The flag hung listlessly in the still night.

"I see the Sun Priest has preceded me."

Her cousin made no answer, but quickened his steps as they reached the door. He stood aside and held up the fine grass mat covering the doorway. "Enter, that my son may live," he said softly as his Honored cousin ducked through the door.

Inside a sacred fire filled the air with acrid smoke. A boy of six summers lay naked on a pallet in the center of the floor. He was curled on his left side and rocked slightly in time with the surging pain. On either side, his mother and aunt sat softly humming the lullabies of their homeland. Cricket Sings walked to the boy and silently shooed the women toward the door. With glances from the corners of their eyes, the young women rose and left the house.

"Yellow Dog," said the old woman softly, "I will need your help."

Yellow Dog entered the house, fear making dark pools of his eyes.

"Go to your son, tell him I am an herb woman. Perhaps my touch will cause pain, but I must do such things to know the proper medicine."

Yellow Dog bent over his son. "My brave one," he whispered. "I know you have much pain. This woman is our cousin and a healer. She has knowledge the Sun Priest lacks."

Cricket Sings walked to the edge of the pallet nearest the boy's head. She bent to smell his breath, then ran a wrinkled hand softly across his brow, noting the dampness and warmth. She looked up at Yellow Dog, who stood near the door of the house. His arms were hanging limply at his sides.

"We will turn the boy onto his back now," she said.

Yellow Dog approached his son and grasped one bent arm. The old woman reached beneath the boy's head to steady it. A low moan escaped between the child's clenched teeth. Quickly they turned the boy on his back. His knees remained bent, pulled tight against his chest. Cricket Sings slid one hand carefully down the boy's body and forced it between his thigh and belly. She felt the hardness of the evil inside.

"How long since he has eaten?" she asked, withdrawing her hand.

"Yesterday, on the trail."

"Does he drink?"

"Since we got here last night he has done nothing but lie upon this pallet and rock."

"He is a brave Warrior," the old woman said in a voice deliberately loud enough for the boy and the women outside to hear. "Many men would have cried like a child, but this boy has borne his pain bravely in silence." She moved her hand to the boy's forehead, once again judging the warmth. "Let us step into the cool night for a moment," she said softly to Yellow Dog.

They rose and left the house. She nodded to the two frightened women waiting outside, who hurried through the door to resume their vigil.

"Come," the old woman said, taking her cousin by the elbow and drawing him away from the house. "It is cold and I do not want your wife to hear."

Yellow Dog followed her to a pallet near the fire. Cricket Sings sank to a squatting position with an audible creak from her knees. Yellow Dog immediately sat beside her.

"The boy is very sick, as you know," she began. "He has an evil in his belly, but there are many kinds of these evils. The worst kill both young and old, while lesser evils take only the weak. This boy is strong and that is good. Does he have the running at the bowels?"

"No, as I said before, he has done nothing but lie there since last night. Once he asked his mother for a bowl in which to make water."

"Some evils of this type turn the bowels soft and run away. But there is one kind which keeps everything inside and kills. I do not know which this is. I have medicine to calm the boy and lessen pain, but I cannot say for sure that he will live."

Yellow Dog's head sank down and he lifted his hands to cover his face. "He is my best son," the old man muttered. "I taught him to hunt as my father taught me. I had no sons by my first wife, only two by this woman and the other has poor eyes. He will never be a Warrior."

"We must decide on the medicine," prompted the herb woman.

"Could you give a medicine which would cause the running at the bowels and thus get rid of the evil?" He looked up hopefully.

"No," she replied. "If he has the other kind of evil such medicine could kill him. The potion to calm the boy is the only help I can offer."

"Then let us do this medicine," Yellow Dog said softly. "I do not like to watch my son dying so bravely. The Sun Priest had no comfort to offer."

As he spoke, Cricket Sings pulled her medicine bag from his shoulder, holding the opening toward the light of the fire. She peered inside, looking for a particular packet of herbs. Pushing aside two larger packets of birthing medicine, she removed a small object wrapped in white deerskin from the bottom of the bag. She also took out a rough stone mano and flat metate with which to grind the medicine. Opening the precious bundle, the old woman set a pinch of dried herbs on the grinding stone. She refolded the package and put it back inside the medicine bag, then rolled the dried leaves between the mano and metate, checking the consistency of the resulting powder with a fingertip.

"Now," she said in a powerful voice, "I need a small bowl of boiling water and a hollow stem of grass."

Yellow Dog called softly to his wife in the Northern language, then went to find a suitable piece of grass. The wife came from the door of the house carrying a small bowl. From a large pot bubbling at the edge of the fire the young woman dipped water into the bowl using a bottle gourd. With downcast eyes the mother gave the bowl to Cricket Sings, who shook the powdered herb into the water, then stirred the mixture with the hollow grass stem handed to her by Yellow Dog. She murmured the medicine song while she stirred. In the firelight her face was a mask of wrinkles, reflecting the wisdom gained in a long life.

"Mother," she said to the young woman. "Hold your son's head in your lap and offer him the grass straw. Tell him in a soft voice that this liquid will quiet his pain and give him sleep."

The young mother nodded nervously, took the bowl, and returned to her son's side. Yellow Dog resumed his place next to Cricket Sings.

"I will go home to my bed now," she said. For the first time there was weariness in her voice. "Come for me in the morning and we will see if this has been the proper medicine." She stood, shouldered her bag, and limped into the night.

CHAPTER TWO
The First Dream

Morning arrived with a rumble of thunder to the west. Cricket Sings saw the grey, lowering sky through the door as she rolled onto her back and raised her arms over her head to stretch. Soon Yellow Dog would come, and a bit of corn porridge would taste good. She sat up at the edge of the pallet, reaching for her deerskin overdress as protection against the morning dampness which made the devils jump in her joints. Doe Eyes, Wolf Hunter and the children were gone. Perhaps they had left early to work in the fields. A wooden comb sat on the floor next to the pallet. The old woman unbraided the left side of her hair, combed it carefully and wove a new, smooth braid, then did the same on the other side.

She picked up a shallow bowl and went outside, dipped hot water from the large jug at the edge of the fire, then added a little to cool it from a storage jug near the door of the house. She splashed her face and neck with the warm water, rotating an index finger in each ear. Next she walked along the path behind her house to the neighborhood toilet, where she emptied her bladder. When she returned to the fire, she splashed the rest of the water from the bowl onto her pubic area. Bodily needs tended, the old woman curled on a mat near the smoldering fire. Cricket Sings saw the dish left from cooking the morning porridge. When she looked

13

inside there was just enough for an old woman's breakfast. Adding a little water from the hot water pot, she stirred the rich mixture of coarse-ground corn and wild seeds and set the bowl on the coals to warm. When it was steaming, she spooned the cereal from the bowl into her mouth with a smooth wooden paddle. Setting the empty bowl at her side, she stood and hobbled into the house. She pulled back a skin covering the grain storage pit and selected a smaller bag woven of plant fibers from the bags of grain buried in a large basket. Pulling open the drawstring at the mouth of the bag, she removed several small dried flowers. The morning was appropriate for yellow flower tea. She tightened the mouth of the bag, replaced it in the pit, then rummaged in her medicine pouch for the small grinding stones. When the yellow flowers and leaves had been ground to a fine powder, she sprinkled it into her drinking bowl. She emerged from the house, bowl in hand, to find Kills the Bear squatting near the fire.

"Kills the Bear, how are you this morning?" she asked in a cheerful voice.

"I have come for the birthing medicine. My wife is having pains and her aunt says the baby will be born by nightfall."

"Ah, I knew her time would be soon. The medicine is here in my pouch. Fill this bowl with hot water for tea and I will fetch what your woman needs."

She handed Kills the Bear her bowl and returned to the house. Several birthing packets were always ready for expectant mothers. The soothing combination of herbs was chewed to hasten birth and decrease bleeding. She gave Kills the Bear a comforting smile as she placed the medicine in his hand.

"This will help your wife in her work. Morning Cloud is a strong girl and her belly is big. You may have a son by tonight. Give her a pinch of these leaves to chew when the pain gets bad and send a runner with news of the baby if it arrives before I do. If there is trouble or if the birthing goes on past evening I will help."

"Thank you, old woman," said Kills the Bear over his shoulder as he hurried down the road.

Cricket Sings returned to her seat at the edge of the fire and sipped her yellow flower tea. She watched the road to the south and soon saw Yellow Dog approaching. From his walk, she knew that the boy still lived, for it was not a dejected walk but rather a careful and deliberate stepping. She sighed. The boy was still very sick.

"Ho, cousin," she called out. "The morning is here and your son remains among the living."

"How do you know this?" Yellow Dog asked, his face puzzled.

Cricket Sings shook her head, careful not to reveal the source of such mysterious knowledge.

"The pain still walks in his belly," Yellow Dog continued. "But he slept this morning. His forehead is cool."

"As I expected." Although she had thought the boy might die during the early morning hours, the old woman did not want her cousin to lose faith in her remedies. Sometimes faith was the most important ingredient in a medicine. "Sit and have a sip of tea and we will talk for a moment, then we will walk to see the boy and perhaps you will sleep. There will be another night to watch over Wounded Deer."

"I am very tired," Yellow Dog admitted, shutting his eyelids slowly. Then his eyes opened. "But one cannot do less for a child." He sat on the ground next to Cricket Sings and accepted the bowl of tea. "This is good tea in a fine bowl, cousin. Is there a new potter in the City?"

"I received that bowl in payment of a debt." She smiled inside, knowing that she had reminded Yellow Dog of his own debt.

"The Basket Maker has begun weaving mats to hang in your door and windows and my other son will deliver them when they are finished."

Cricket Sings nodded in answer. The gift was her due. "I know some potters," she said. "You may want to trade with them while you are here. Since you are staying until after the Celebration of the Sun there will be plenty of time for trading. You could become a rich man."

"The people of the North City do not have such well-made tools and ornaments. They have copper to trade, but the Warriors are difficult, much given to anger and killing."

Cricket Sings refilled the tea bowl with hot water and handed it to Yellow Dog. "Certainly they are cordial to traders?"

He nodded his thanks. "The Northern hospitality is not like our own. My wife's brother told me of emissaries from an eastern people who came to trade for copper. The deer hunting was not good that year and it is said that the Northern people ate their visitors."

The old woman turned to her cousin with wide open eyes. "You are serious, Yellow Dog?"

"This is not something I saw with my own eyes, only gossip around the campfire. The brother claims that he has taken part in feasts after warfare when the bodies of powerful enemies were cooked and eaten, but that is a custom among many people."

"There was no war, the emissaries came only to trade?"

"That is my understanding."

"Our Priests sacrifice Ordinaries each year at festivals, and at times of special need the People volunteer for sacrifice. It is well known that the Sun Priests eat the flesh of such Holy Ones."

"Yes, but that is a ceremony! You know the flesh of a sacrifice takes on the character of the Gods."

Suddenly there was a silence between them. Cricket Sings spoke first.

"Let us go to see your boy, then I have some errands. I will be telling stories again tonight, will you join us? Perhaps my daughter could watch the boy while your family comes to our fire?"

"I do not like to leave my son when he is in pain, but I will speak with my wife and decide in the evening." As he said this, Yellow Dog stood and stretched. No longer was he the slim boy Cricket Sings had known as a young woman. Now he was stocky and well-muscled, with quick movements and the inner power of Warrior status. Like many older Warriors, Yellow Dog had turned to trade in middle life. His first marriage to an older woman had produced no children. After she died Yellow Dog had begun to travel the Great River. In the land of the Northerners he had met his pretty wife.

Cricket Sings stood slowly with a grunt, then walked to the door of her house and pulled out the medicine bag. "I have not gone anywhere without my bag for years," she explained to Yellow Dog.

"I always think of you with that bag under your arm," he replied. "It seems to have grown onto your side from so much carrying."

"I no longer have a husband to keep me warm, although I must admit this bag is a poor substitute for such pleasures." She laughed softly, remembering her lover Sand Crane.

"Would you take another husband if a handsome young man were to court you?"

"These days I worry more about handsome old men," Cricket Sings replied with a twinkle in her eye. "They all have their eyes on the girls." Suddenly her face was sad. "There has been only one lover for me, Yellow Dog. Besides, I have a daughter with a strong husband who hunts. We grow corn and trade for everything else we need. I am past the age when Moon calls me and those urges are now dim."

The cousins walked the road which ran between the peaked-roof houses of the People. They stopped for a moment to watch a new house being built next to Kills the Bear's, but after an impatient sigh from Yellow Dog Cricket Sings hurried away toward Basket Maker's. After the morning bowl of porridge families were working. Farmers hurried toward the fields, each carrying a hoe. Warriors were on their way to the hills or river bottom to hunt deer. Ahead at the side of the road Cricket Sings saw the large, well-cared-for house of Crow Eater, the younger brother of her beloved husband Sand Crane. Crow Eater was a stone worker as his brother had been, and sat in the sunshine chipping his beautiful tools.

"Let's talk with Crow Eater for a moment," the old woman said. "I am in need of a new knife."

"Perhaps I could bring you one from the North," Yellow Dog began, but Cricket Sings had walked ahead.

"Good morning, brother of my husband," she called.

The young man at the fireside looked up, smiling when he saw his visitors.

"Cricket Sings, I have not seen you for many days and wondered whether you were well. It is good to see you."

"I need a knife and you do the best flint work in the City, my young brother."

"Since Sand Crane died I have taken his place," Crow Eater replied, setting aside his tools. "Just a moment, I have a fine piece of stone which you may want me to use for your knife." He rose, taller and slimmer than Yellow Dog. Crow Eater's body lacked the concentration of muscle which marked the Warrior, but his bearing was prideful. "Sit, sit and I will be right back." He disappeared into the house.

Cricket Sings squatted next to the fire. Yellow Dog remained standing and rocked impatiently from foot to foot. The old woman ignored him. She knew that he wanted to know whether or not his son would live and that she might not be able to give him an answer. Crow Eater made noise as he rummaged among his belongings and murmured to someone inside the house. A young woman emerged, clutching a moccasin she had been decorating.

"Cricket Sings!" the girl exclaimed. "I have had the strangest dream!"

The herb woman nodded. Soon to be Winter often had dreams which foretold the future, but the girl did not yet have the wisdom to interpret her special knowledge. "While your husband looks for flints, tell me your dream. I will consider the meaning and speak with you later. My cousin's son has an evil in his belly and we must hurry."

She heard Yellow Dog sigh with relief that they would not be delayed much longer.

"There was a whiteness," Soon to be Winter began. "Not that of light, but the other kind, and I was not myself. My spirit was alone and feared for the life of another. I cannot say how far I wandered, but at the end of the journey I came to a high hill. I flew to the top where men were feasting. When I approached the fire a man turned to me. His face was horrible, smeared with blood." Soon to be Winter stopped, then spoke more slowly. "I awoke crying and my husband said I called out in a language he did not know."

"That is so," added Crow Eater as he pushed aside the doorskin and emerged from the house. "I was afraid for her. I do not like evil visions in the night."

The old woman felt uneasy. The dream was clearly a bad omen. "You are right, this is a strange dream and will need much interpretation. Will you come to hear my stories tonight?"

"Of course!" the young couple answered together. They looked at each other and smiled before Crow Eater continued. "We enjoy your stories. I only wish that my brother had lived long enough to tell his."

"Yes," said Cricket Sings in a thoughtful voice. "That man would have told good stories." She was silent for a moment, remembering the past. "Let me see what you have in your hand."

"I have two good rocks here, although one has better lines. Since you will be using the knife, I will let you choose the piece you like."

The herb woman took the stones offered by Crow Eater and examined each carefully, noting the preliminary fracture lines and the weight and balance. "I will take this one," she said, holding out one stone to Crow Eater.

"A fine choice," he answered. "The other has a good color, but I thought perhaps you would want a knife to cut with as well as look at."

"I am in no hurry for the knife." She gave him the other piece of flint. "Work the stone and when you have finished we will agree on a price. In the meantime, perhaps some corn or fish would taste good at your fire?"

"Either would be most welcome."

Cricket Sings rose from her squatting position and they all heard her knees creak. "I do not only hop like a cricket, my body sings, too," she joked. "Thank you for your pleasant company. We will gather in the evening."

Yellow Dog was already walking down the road. Crow Eater called out after the cousins as they left.

"We must talk about trading for some copper. I would like to make ornaments this winter."

"I can get you the copper, we will talk later," shouted Yellow Dog. He took Cricket Sings by the elbow and tried to hurry her down the road.

"Cousin," she said testily. "I may be old and crippled, but I can walk under my own power and will do so at my own speed!" With this reprimand, she set off down the road at a pace even faster than Yellow Dog's. Caught unaware, he had to hurry to catch up.

"Crazy old woman," she heard him mutter behind her.

Basket Maker was sitting in the shade cast by the walls of his house and Cricket Sings saw a delicate mat taking shape under his skillful fingers. He looked up as they approached.

"The women are inside, although the boy is sleeping."

The old woman turned to her cousin, who was slightly out of breath. "Wait here," she said in a strong voice, then turned and entered the house.

A woman sat on either side of the boy. Even in daylight the two appeared almost identical in size and features. They both looked so Northern that the herb woman could not tell them apart.

"Mother!" she said loudly.

SIMMS LIBRARY
ALBUQUERQUE ACADEMY

Immediately, one woman jumped up and took two steps toward her, maintaining a respectful distance.

"I am the mother," she answered in a soft voice with a lisping Northern accent.

"And your name?"

"I am Shade of the Tree, but my husband calls me Shade because he says my name is too long."

"Shade of the Tree is a most beautiful name, you should stretch such words to their full length, like a song. How is your son?"

"Please, see for yourself, he is sleeping. We kept watch and all night he sipped the medicine. This is his first sleep since the evil caught him."

Cricket Sings walked to the pallet and bent over the boy. She saw that he was indeed sleeping and not in a coma. His breath came softly between parted lips and the hair was damp at his forehead. She ran her wise old hand across his cheek. The boy's skin felt cool and slightly moist. Although Wounded Deer lay on his side with his knees bent, the legs were not drawn tightly to his chest as they had been the night before. The healer looked up into the faces of the anxious women.

"The boy is much better, I think. In the night these evils become worse and then with the coming of light they hide. I think he may be sick again tonight, but he will probably live."

The two sisters were excited by this news and chattered like birds in the Northern language, then ran outside to tell the men. Once more Cricket Sings bent over the boy. She pressed her hand onto his forehead and felt the strong life within his body. He looked very much like his father. She was glad the boy would live. Rising slowly and with effort, she went outside to the expectant family.

"I will give you more medicine," she said in answer to the unspoken questions in their eyes. "Yellow Dog, you saw me grind the herbs. Do you remember how much water to use? This medicine must be the proper strength."

Yellow Dog nodded. Cricket Sings lowered herself to a seated position on a mat and extracted the leather-wrapped calmative from her medicine pouch. She measured out a good amount of the drug and dumped the mixture into a bowl offered by Shade of the Tree.

"The water must be boiling," the herb woman instructed. "That is most important! Give some to the boy when he wakes. Do not offer him food until he complains of hunger, and then give him only broth."

"Thank you, grandmother," the young woman murmured.

"You must come to hear my stories tonight," the old woman commanded, replacing her tool kit in her medicine pouch. "When I am gone there must be young ones who remember. I will send my daughter to sing for the boy while you are gone. Bring the other children." She stood, adjusted her heavy bag to a comfortable position on her shoulder and marched briskly down the road toward the corn fields.

CHAPTER THREE
One Eye

The morning was hot and overhanging clouds threatened rain. Cricket Sings was thirsty and wished she had made a less dramatic exit, but asking for a cup of water would have spoiled the supernatural image she wanted to project. She walked between the huts of the Ordinaries now. These People were poorer than those living closer to the central City. Their huts were small and many had holes in the thatching so that there were bad leaks during rainstorms. Ordinaries lacked a family trade by birth or bad fortune and labored building holy hills or in the charnel houses in return for a dole of corn from the Sun King.

She stopped at the fire of Carries Stones, who worked with his two older children in the borrow pits of the City, hauling dirt for the holy hills. A younger daughter, known as Little One, had stepped in the fire, burning her foot and leg badly. Although the family could not pay, the herb woman had been called because it was known that she did not like children to suffer. The foot was healing well now, but the child had been hurt in spirit as well as body by the accident.

"Hello, my Little One," Cricket Sings called out in her cheeriest grandmother voice. "Are you keeping watch over the fire for your family?"

"I try to keep a small fire burning so we can have our porridge in the evening," the child replied politely. She was sitting on a torn mat, her hair in tangles and her face smeared with dirt. Although several summers older than Wounded Deer, Little One was about the same size.

"They leave you alone all day?" the old woman questioned.

"We must work to eat and since I cannot walk to the borrow pit I must keep my own company. It is good that my brothers share their corn with a weakling such as me."

"Where is your mother?" The old woman opened her bag and removed a special ointment made of bear grease and soothing plants.

"She has gone to a small corn field which no one wanted. Mother planted a few squash seeds that a farmer dropped on his way to the fields and also some corn saved from our food. The field is at the farthest edge of the City." Little One shook her head at the thought of such a long walk.

Carefully, Cricket Sings unwrapped the skin tied about the child's foot. The parents had not thought the injury serious until it began to fester. With care, washing, and a bear grease coating to keep out dirt the wounds had begun to heal. Now only two areas lacked new pink skin. One was at the outside of the ankle, but the other was on the pad of the foot and the child would not be able to walk until it healed.

"Have you been soaking this foot in a bowl of warm water each night as I instructed?" the old woman asked in a stern voice.

"Yes, Honored Woman. Even though my mother is tired in the evening she helps me with the water."

"Your foot looks good. Soon you will be able to run and play again."

"No," the child corrected. "Soon I will be able to help my father and brothers in their work. We will have a larger ration of corn. Perhaps I will get plump!"

Cricket Sings nodded, but secretly she did not think children should work. Yet, when one's father had no trade it was necessary to earn a living at an early age. Briskly the old woman applied a coating of bear grease from the small pot before rewrapping the foot.

"Not too long now, Little One, until you will once again be your father's helper."

"Will I see you tomorrow, Cricket Sings?" the child asked eagerly, hungry for company.

"Perhaps, if I am in this part of the City. In two days the Celebration of the Sun will be held and I have much to do before that time. I have to go to the market and trade for herbs which have come here by river for this special occasion." At the look of dismay which crossed the small face, Cricket Sings changed her mind. "Yes, yes, I am an old woman but I will walk down here to see a friend. My Little One, I must hurry now." With a wave, she picked up her bag and walked down the road between the corn fields. She knew her destination was near. Soon she recognized the woven grass sunhats of her daughter and son-in-law bobbing up and down as they cultivated corn. Son was propped in his cradleboard, sleeping soundly. Behind her father, tiny Daughter poked at the ground with a stick and babbled in her own language. She was not yet at the age for naming, but already it was apparent that in quantity of speech the child resembled her Great-aunt Running Water.

"Hello Doe Eyes, Wolf Hunter," the old woman called to get the couple's attention. "How grows the corn?"

"Honored Mother." Doe Eyes turned with a bow and a smile. "The corn would like a little rain, but this year the weeds are not too bad. Perhaps we will be able to go on our trip after the Celebration."

Each summer the family traveled to the bluffs east of the City to camp and gather berries and herbs for use during the winter.

"Have you been visiting?" Doe Eyes went on. "You were not in the house until just before dawn, so I did not wake you this morning."

"Give me that hoe, child, and rest. It does an old woman good to hoe in the Sun."

Doe Eyes handed the shell hoe to her mother and knelt beside the cradleboard. She nuzzled her baby's sleeping face tenderly and he whimpered and opened his eyes. Doe Eyes sat beside him, tipped the cradleboard across her lap, and gave the child her full breast.

"Well, Mother, I am interested in gossip. Who were you out to see last night?"

"What a daughter, you have no more manners than . . ."

"Than you!" the impudent girl finished.

Cricket Sings turned to her son-in-law. "This wife needs a beating," she said in a stern voice.

Wolf Hunter, used to the banter between his wife and her mother, laughed and replied, "You have the hoe in your hand, Honored Mother, you beat her!"

Cricket Sings stepped into the row Doe Eyes had been hoeing and chopped at the weeds. Soon she began to perspire and stopped for a drink from the water jug. The sweat felt good on her skin. Throwing her overdress down near Doe Eyes, who was drowsing with the baby in her arms, the old woman went back to work. After loosening the earth and chopping weeds between several rows, she turned and handed the hoe to Wolf Hunter.

"You are a good farmer, for a Warrior."

"I am proud of our field, but Doe Eyes is the farmer. I help only when the seeds grow too fast for her. Come and see the squash plants and bottle gourds."

After admiring the progress of the garden, the old woman prepared to leave. "Tell my daughter that I will be sure to save all the gossip for her."

"I will do that, Mother," answered Wolf Hunter with a smile.

Cricket Sings bent over her sleeping daughter and grandson. They were very beautiful. Doe Eyes' slender hand lay next to her son's face, fingers stretched tenderly over his fat cheek. The old woman put on her overdress and picked up her bag. She stroked Daughter's soft hair before turning to Wolf Hunter. "I am going to the plaza and then I must see Kills the Bear's wife. She is birthing her first child today."

"Kills the Bear thinks it will be a son?"

"All men think their firstborn will be a son!" she called back to Wolf Hunter as she left.

Soon the old woman smelled the wetness of the ponds ahead. Rushes grew thickly along the shallow edges of the lake and she saw birds of many colors. Hungry fish made swirls on the surface of the water. Fishermen, who made their living on the many rivers and lakes of the area, kept fish too small to eat in baskets and later dumped them into the lakes of the City. After the evening meal, families often walked to the lake to fish. Now naked children were laughing and splashing in the water, waving to Cricket Sings as she walked past. Ahead was the house of her sister, Running Water. As a girl Running Water had been married to a very old Warrior and served only to keep his bed warm. When he died there were no children and the house and cornfields of his family went to Running Water. Later she had married a Warrior and now they had two near-grown daughters.

"Running Water, are you inside?" Cricket Sings called out.

"Here I am, sister," answered a familiar voice as a plump, middle-aged woman emerged from behind the house. "I have been to the toilet. I knew you would be here this morning. Isn't the Celebration exciting this year? We made the girls new dresses; perhaps they will catch the eye of a Warrior and make a marriage. How are Doe Eyes and the others?" Running Water never tired of talk.

"Hush, sister, everything is fine. I am going to the plaza to see what the traders have brought and perhaps make a deal or two. Would you like to walk along with me?"

"Oh no, oh no, I have too much to do here. We are having a small feast in honor of the Sun, you know. Well, of course you know, you are invited. Could you bring some of that yellow flower tea you have been making and perhaps some corn breads? We will have the venison and we dug some roots, although the berries are not yet ripe. Look at that strange bird, it is late in the year . . ."

"Well, then, I am leaving," Cricket Sings said abruptly. She knew she would have to walk away swiftly to escape her sister's web of speech. "Are you coming to the stories tonight?"

"Of course, sister, of course. Soon it will be time for me to tell stories and one must know how it is done. You give yours such dignity." Suddenly Running Water bent to the ground. "Well, here is that piece of sinew I was looking for the other day. How did it get here?"

When Running Water turned to put the sinew in a safer place, the herb woman saw her chance and edged away from the fire, then turned and hobbled as fast as she could toward the palisade gate. "Goodbye, sister," she shouted so that Running Water would know she was gone and not babble foolishly to no one.

The palisade was made of logs placed upright in great trenches surrounding the central City. Narrow gaps spaced at intervals allowed the People to enter or leave the great plaza, where the business of the City was carried on. Places of worship and the homes of spiritual leaders were located on mounds scattered about the plaza.

As Cricket Sings passed between the tall logs of the southern gate, she saw the twin Death Mounds and shivered. Her own family's death mounds were near her house and had never been fearsome, but for Cricket Sings these death hills of the Sun Priests vibrated with evil auras. Malevolent spirits seemed to hover over the black charnel house squatted on top of the pyramid-shaped hill. The other hill was cone-shaped. It was there that the bodies were buried after the flesh had rotted in the charnel house. The scent of decay which emanated from both hills reminded the People of their mortality. Cricket Sings felt her own death close behind her.

She passed between the two mounds and sighed with relief. Ahead were the bright flags and tents of the festival. Men were playing chunky, gambling on the outcome. One man rolled a disk-shaped stone along a smooth path, then he and an opponent followed, throwing spears where each thought the stone would stop. The winner was the one who came closer to predicting the place at which the stone would slow and roll onto its side. Near the chunky players another group of men were gambling with bones painted red and black, trying to guess how many the others held in each hand.

Walking closer to the central plaza, Cricket Sings lifted her head to sniff the delicious aromas of baking corn and roasting meat. She stopped at a small stand where a grinning but toothless grandmother sold crisp corn breads and traded a few pinches of yellow flower tea for a large bread.

"Thank you, thank you," the old woman said through fluttering lips as she stored the small package of tea safely in her pocket.

The herb woman turned away and hobbled down the street. She was looking for the other herbalists now, they would be setting up stands from which to sell their medicines. Ahead a green flag flapped atop a tall pole. Cricket Sings hobbled faster, waving one hand over her head in excitement. The very old woman who sat on the ground at the foot of the flagpole had taught her the birthing medicine. In her youth Magic Swan had been very beautiful, but an unsuccessful suitor had put out her eye in a jealous rage. Now the lid hung over an empty socket and the horror of the wound disappeared into fine wrinkles at the edge of One Eye's face. She had never married, instead supporting herself and the orphans she called her children by dispensing herbs and attending at births.

"Honored Woman," Cricket Sings said softly as she stepped in front of her friend. "I have come to visit with you."

One Eye turned her face toward the voice. "Ah, it is you, child. My other eye is blind now, but I would know you even in sleep."

Cricket Sings squatted beside her friend, laying the medicine bag on the ground at her side. "How are you, Honored One? You look thinner this year."

"Shh," the old woman said, reaching a claw-like hand for Cricket Sings' arm and pulling her closer. "I have an evil in my breast that will not heal and my legs shake when I try to walk. I will not be here next year. You must take my place. I will give you my flag . . ." One Eye's voice faltered. She cleared her throat. "I heard that you are telling stories."

"Yes, Honored One. Please come to my house tonight, ask your daughters to bring you."

"I would like to hear your stories. Mine were told long ago and now the children repeat them."

"I wish I had a medicine for the sore in your breast, Old One."

"Well, I have lived a long time, had many children and much love. I regret never having known a husband, but no man could warm my old bones now."

"Any number of young men would be proud to sleep close to you on winter nights," Cricket Sings flattered gently.

The older woman opened her mouth wide in a gap-toothed grin, then changed the subject.

"I have heard of a new medicine for the sickness that makes the ankles swell and breathing difficult."

"It's a pity you do not have that trouble. What is your recipe?"

"In the spring, very early, there is a small round leaf which pokes up where the ground is moist. Not near a lake, but if there is water in the woods, that is a good place. I call it the dog-paw plant because the leaf resembles a dog's paw print in mud. Dry and powder this leaf and give the ailing one a pinch of the powder to place between the lip and gum each morning."

"I will look for this dog-paw plant, learned one. I also have a new medicine, a calmative. I mix the flat leaf that grows near oak trees with the birthing medicine moss and grind them to powder. From this brew tea with boiling water for the patient to sip. This medicine helped a boy with evil in the belly last night, but it works only for lesser evils."

"There will never be cures for bad evils," said One Eye sadly.

The women sat together in friendly silence. Around them swirled the busy festival. Bright flags called attention to the stands of Shamen, Priests and Herbalists. Cricket Sings and One Eye were facing west and as the breeze became stronger and the flags began to wave and snap, the younger woman saw storm clouds moving toward the City.

"One Eye, rain promised by the sky this morning is approaching. We should move to a place where you will not get wet."

"No, let me sit here and feel the rain on my face. I can no longer see the clouds and soon I will know a cold which does not go away."

Cricket Sings nodded. "I respect you, Honored One. A young wife is birthing her first son today and I must see her. Will you walk to the Ceremony of the Sun two mornings from now?"

"No, I do not think I will go this year since I cannot see the Sun's coming."

"Old One," Cricket Sings said in a voice which was suddenly strained and low. "I fear that is not wise. The Sun Priests check to see that all of the Honored and Warriors attend the Ceremony. The families of those who do not attend are held in disfavor from that time on."

"I have many children, it is true."

"My dear friend, two years ago the family three houses from my own fell into disfavor. The old grandfather was ill and his legs were not working at all. He did not attend the Ceremony and before the next Moon closed his daughter and her family were declared bastards and imposters. They were stripped of all their property and now labor among the Ordinaries."

"I am sorry to hear of this. Such news rarely reaches our small village. I do not understand why Sun Priests should be concerned with one old man."

"It was more than one old man. Whispers have been heard that the Sun Priests are corrupt, that they keep the Sun their prisoner so they may do whatever they wish. They not only have the women they desire, but also precious ornaments and sacred foods. Each

feast day they sacrifice Ordinaries, and this was not done in my
youth. It is said that the Priests eat the flesh of the sacrifices, not
to commune with the Gods, but because they like the taste."

"You are speaking treason," One Eye said harshly. "Do not
think such words will not spread. If your life has value, you will talk
no more of such things."

"It is not my life, but the faith of all the People who look to this
City for communion with the Gods."

"Who else knows you have such thoughts?"

"No one but you," Cricket Sings replied.

"From time to time I have heard rumors. Not facts, you understand, but idle gossip that the people of the North are cannibals.
I have always thought of such tales as inventions around the
campfire, but you give them new meaning. Perhaps I will ask one
of my sons to investigate when we return home after the Ceremony."

"By doing so you may endanger your own life, as well as all your
orphans."

"My friend, we both know my life is not worth a year. If evil is
among the People we must raise alarm. Grandmothers have a duty
to pass on the knowledge of ancestors."

"Thank you, One Eye, for sharing my problem. I have asked
questions and told stories most carefully so that no one would
know of my interest. Here is the rain." As she spoke, a grey curtain
descended across the plaza. The colorful trappings of the chunky
players suddenly hung limp and bedraggled. Men ran toward the
Men's Houses around the perimeter of the Plaza while the women
and children scurried in every direction to retrieve belongings
before they became wet. Cricket Sings stood and pulled the back
of her loose overdress up over her head, tucking her face down
behind it so the rain would not blow into her eyes. She touched
One Eye on the shoulder, then clutched the medicine bag tightly
under one arm so it would not be lost and limped toward the
palisade gate. When she turned to look back, the plaza was nearly
empty, the skin huts of the merchants deserted and dripping. One
Eye sat alone, very small and old, her wrinkled face turned up to
the storm.

CHAPTER FOUR
Prophecy

As Cricket Sings walked home through the rain she felt the devils dancing in her hip. The streets were deserted outside the palisade, but smoke poured in a thin stream from the smoke hole in the roof of her house and she knew that Doe Eyes and her family were safe from the rain. The old woman pushed back the skin flap and entered the house. She stood by the door while her wet clothes dripped.

"Hello, Mother, you are very wet!" Doe Eyes said in greeting.

"I went to the plaza to see the festival. One Eyes was there and we talked. Before I knew, the storm was upon us."

"One Eye! Oh, mother, how is she?" Doe Eyes sat back on her heels. "I remember when she told her stories and they were very beautiful. Did she have any new recipes?"

Cricket Sings' eyes had adjusted to the dim light inside the house and she could now see that her daughter had been grinding corn near the fire. The baby slept in his cradleboard leaning against the wall and Daughter was playing with a ragged doll made of cornhusks.

The old woman's voice was thick. "One Eye will not be here next year. She has an evil in her breast. We have been friends for so long, I do not know what I will do without her wise counsel." Cricket Sings sniffled into the shoulder of her very wet overdress.

Doe Eyes saw her mother's need, jumped up, and circled the old woman's shoulder with a loving arm. "Mother, come close to the fire and take off your wet clothes. I am sorry to hear of the illness of our friend; she is a good woman."

Cricket Sings slumped onto a mat near the fire. She pulled the soaked overdress off over her head and tossed it into a corner, then removed her damp moccasins and wiggled her toes in front of the fire's heat.

"This feels very good, daughter. By chance, is there a bit of tea?"

"Being most dutiful, I had the water and yellow flower herbs ready for your return, Mother. Will you make me a bowl?"

Cricket Sings ceremoniously prepared two bowls of tea, then resumed her position on the mat. She pushed one bowl up next to Doe Eyes, the other toward her own place.

"Where is your husband?"

"Gone to the Men's House to talk with his brothers about hunting and fishing. We must begin to dry fish and meat soon or the winter will bring hunger. He said that Morning Cloud is bearing her first son for Kills the Bear, is this so?"

"Kills the Bear came for the birthing medicine this morning. I must go and see Morning Cloud when I am warm and dry."

"I will hang your overdress here," said Doe Eyes. She stood and hung the dripping garment on a peg near the door. "Would you like to wear my cloak? I have no need for it; the children and I will be here because I am baking corn breads."

"I had a delicious corn bread at the festival," the old woman began, then thought the better of leaving a statement like that. "But not as good as yours!" she finished and was rewarded by her daughter's smile. "Where is your cloak? I will need my second-best moccasins, too."

Cricket Sings rummaged in the corner of the house farthest from the door. She pulled out first one moccasin, then the other as Doe Eyes unfolded a long skin cloak.

"Here you are, Mother. Something to keep you warm."

The cloak was made of tanned deerskin. The old woman stood and her daughter laid the cloak across her bent shoulders. It reached almost to the ground. Around the neck and hem dyed porcupine quills were sewn in designs which had a special meaning for Doe Eyes. She had made the cloak from skins Wolf Hunter had left on the doorstep as a sign that he wanted her for his wife.

Cricket Sings sat on the mat-covered floor and pulled on her old moccasins, clucking her tongue at a thin spot on the sole of one.

In a few swift gulps she drank her tea, then stood and adjusted the beautiful cloak.

"I look more like a bride than a poor herb woman in all this finery. Well, I am off to see the arrival of another first son. Take good care of our own little ones. Perhaps we should move some of these mats. I have invited many people for my story tonight and with the rain we will have to sit inside the house. I would prefer the stars," she muttered as an afterthought. She turned and lifted the doorskin, noting that the rain had diminished in intensity, but did not appear to be ending. "Well, I am going now," she repeated.

"Go, then, Mother. I will move the mats to make room for your visitors."

"Oh, I almost forgot. I promised Yellow Dog that you would sit with his son so the rest of the family might hear the stories."

"You will care for the children?"

"If Wolf Hunter is not here I will keep them at my side."

"Good. I will not mind visiting my small cousin. You can remind me of the story later so that I will be able to tell my own grandchildren."

"Thank you, daughter," the old woman said as she went into the rain. She carefully covered the door, then walked south on the road to the house of Morning Cloud's family. The young couple lived with her mother and sisters. A brother already slept in the Men's House. As she approached, she saw Kills the Bear squatting in the mud near the door. He looked up sorrowfully.

"They will not let me stay with my wife."

"This is women's work," she consoled. "Soon your wife will give you a son and you will hold him up to the rain. Perhaps he will dream of water when he reaches manhood and remember this day in his name."

The young man nodded sadly and resumed his position. "I will wait here," he said in a determined voice.

The old woman entered the house. The mother, sisters and aunts of Morning Cloud were gathered about the young woman, who was kneeling on a pallet. She alternately worked to push the baby out of her belly, then rested as the urgency abated for a moment. Her face contorted once more. Cricket Sings shooed the other women to the far side of the house, flapping her hands at them, then turned to Morning Cloud.

"Did you chew the birthing medicine?"

The young mother nodded a vigorous yes, accompanied by a grunt of effort. She reached beneath her skirt and Cricket Sings knew immediately what she wanted. The old woman looked around the hut, then grabbed a sash that was used to hold back the doorskin in better weather and handed it to Morning Cloud, who tied the dress above her bulging belly. A small dark-haired head could be seen between her legs now and the mother guided the baby up and out in rhythm with her body. As the tiny legs slid out out, the child uttered a short cry.

"A son!" the mother shouted triumphantly.

Kills the Bear burst through the door to see his young wife holding their son. He attempted to take the child from her to offer it to the Gods, not realizing that it was still attached to her body.

"Wait, wait, do not be in such a hurry, Father," Cricket Sings cried, jumping between the new parents. She pointed to the umbilical cord which still pulsed. The baby was crying strongly now and Morning Cloud sank back onto her haunches to rest for a moment. The contractions began again. With the herb woman giving directions in a soft voice, the mother guided the afterbirth from her body.

"Good, you are a wise mother already," Cricket Sings praised.

The infant rested on the mat before its mother, caked with blood and mucus. Morning Cloud reached out to touch her new son's short nose with one finger and smiled despite her tiredness. "He is the son I wanted for you," she said, looking up at Kills the Bear.

"He is our new Warrior," Kills the Bear replied proudly.

Cricket Sings spoke to the mother of Morning Cloud. "We will need the knife of your family."

The woman nodded and turned to the back of the house. Family treasures were stored above their heads on a small wooden platform supported by the roof. She reached up over the edge of the platform and pulled out a small skin case containing the ritual knife used for cutting umbilical cords and sinews with which to tie the cord. The knife was handed to the young mother. The herb woman checked the cord, found it blue and cold, and tied it with a piece of sinew to keep out evil spirits. Finally, the mother cut the cord several inches from the child's belly with a flourish.

"It will dry and fall off," Cricket Sings assured her, pointing to the stump of the cord.

The new grandmother took the afterbirth and draped it over a peg in the wall. When dried, the afterbirth would be the first object placed in the child's medicine bag.

"Now is the time, Father," Morning Cloud said to her husband.

Kills the Bear carefully picked up his firstborn son and went out into the rainy afternoon. All the women except the new mother crowded around the doorway to watch. Chanting the songs of his family in a quiet voice to soothe the chilled and screaming baby, the father offered his son first to the east, where the Sun rises. In turn the child was dedicated to the south, where the Sun is warmest; to the north, home of winter; and finally to the west, region of sunset and death. By the time they entered the house, the women had readied small garments for the child. A new cradleboard rested against a wall. The baby was washed gently with warm water and wrapped in diapers made of woven plant fibers followed by a tiny vest and bunting of softest deerskin. He was then handed to his mother, who bared her breast. The new Warrior began to suck and fill his belly.

"He is a strong man," chirped a young sister of Morning Cloud.

"His member is very large, that is the sign of a powerful hunter," added an aunt.

No one noticed Cricket Sings slipping out the door. It was nearly evening and she had not yet considered the meaning of Soon to be Winter's dream. The evil vision, filled with a sense of tragedy, had been on her mind all day, but now she had time to walk slowly in the rain. She pondered. Perhaps the dream meant that Soon to be Winter, named for the sensations of whiteness which preceded her visions, would not experience the evil alone because she had entered another spirit during the dream. There had been a journey to a hill where men feasted. The Sun Celebration was a time of feasting for all, but men did have special feasts of their own at other times of the year. The horrible mask could be a reflection of good or evil. The Gods often spoke in such riddles. Cricket Sings turned and walked toward her own house. The rain had slackened to a drizzle now and in the west a weak Sun sent fingers of light through holes in the clouds. She thought of One Eye, grieving that the other woman could no longer see the glory of the Sun. As she reached the door of her house, Wolf Hunter was approaching.

"Hello, Mother," he greeted her. "We are planning a hunt tommorrow. Each family will have a haunch of meat to celebrate. I have hoed corn long enough and it is time to feel the hills pulling at my legs and to walk with my brothers."

He allowed Cricket Sings to precede him into the house, holding back the doorskin for her.

"How is the corn bread?" the old woman called out.

"The bread is fine and we have a small squash which I saved from the winter and baked secretly so you would not know," answered Doe Eyes. "Did Kills the Bear get his son?"

"Indeed, he has a fine new Warrior. An aunt said the child's large member is a sign of power in hunting. It may be so, for I also helped birth the father and there is a certain resemblance. Kills the Bear was a little anxious to dedicate the child to the winds, but otherwise the birth went well. Morning Cloud will have many more children."

Wolf Hunter removed his cloak, larger and plainer than the one Cricket Sings wore, and hung it on a peg next to the door. Seeing this, Cricket Sings realized that her daughter's fine cloak was damp.

"I am sorry for getting your cloak wet," she said, removing it and hanging it next to Wolf Hunter's

"Mother," admonished Doe Eyes. "That's what a cloak is made for. You two must be cold, sit here next to the fire and we will eat. See how I have moved the pallets to make room for the stories tonight?"

The two sank to their knees next to Doe Eyes, who was spooning baked squash into bowls. She handed each of them a bowl and a wooden spoon, then took up her own. Wolf Hunter reached toward the rock where freshly baked corn breads were warming at the fireside, picked one up and took an enormous bite.

"Delicious," he said through a full mouth. "Woman, you are a good cook as well as beautiful."

"Of course," answered his wife. "There is nothing else to do but cook when you go off to huddle in that Men's House for hours."

Wolf Hunter smiled at her and went on eating. Cricket Sings remembered her own youth. As the mother of three small children, she too had felt overburdened by the constant round of cooking, sewing and field work.

"The children will grow and soon you will be able to talk with them," she murmured in consolation.

Daughter woke and rolled off the pile of skins on which she had been napping. Doe Eyes jumped up and took the child outdoors. Children could be taught not to wet or soil themselves at an early age, but the utmost diligence was required on the part of the mother. When she returned, the baby was crying in his cradleboard. A sigh escaped between her lips. Cricket Sings heard and looked up, seeing her daughter's tired face.

"Sit, child, and I will tend the boy. Perhaps he would like some squash." She pulled the cradleboard toward her and felt the child's robes with her hand. "He is not wet through, but I believe he has soiled himself," she said. "Phew! Babies smell worse every year." Unwrapping her grandson from the cradleboard, she loosened the baby's soiled clothing and used it to wipe him gently. Then she walked to the door and threw the dirty garments into the mud. She pulled a coarse-woven diaper from those piled in the corner where clothing was stored and redressed the child, who was now screaming with hunger. "Good exercise," she remarked to her son-in-law. "He will be a singer with a voice like that."

Finally, she handed the boy to his mother, who tucked him close to her breast and fed him dabs of squash cooled on the end of her spoon. The baby contorted his tiny face at the strange texture and the family laughed. Doe Eyes gave the boy her breast and the house was filled with the contented hum of a nursing child. Cricket Sings and Wolf Hunter finished their meal in silence, then the old woman rose and left the hut, picking up the boy's soiled clothing. The drizzle was over and sunset had begun, leftover storm clouds breaking the sun into colorful streams. Mist hung over the Big Lake. The old woman walked alone to the toilet pit where she emptied her bladder and bowels. Then she carred the dirty diaper to a stream which ran behind her house and rinsed the garment carefully. Her neighbors were emerging from their houses, calling and waving to friends or relatives. Many wore colorful dance costumes and walked toward the plaza. The first of the Sun Dances would be held the next afternoon and these men and women would practice their steps during the dusk.

Near the creek three small boys were throwing rocks at one of the yellow dogs which scavenged at the fringes of the City. Cricket Sings laughed as a stick hit the dog, sending him howling behind the Burial Hill. The boys chased after the dog, hoping to catch and kill it. Such a meal would be a great treat. She saw Soon to be Winter walking slowly toward the palisade, dressed in her dancing finery.

"Dreamer of omens," the old woman called, waving one hand. "Wait for an old woman who cannot match the speed of your young legs."

Soon to be Winter turned with a smile. "Cricket Sings, it is good to see you. I thought you had forgotten my dream and it is lonely to have an omen which no one shares."

"Next time you will know better than to doubt my concern. I have been busy today, but your wisdom is of great importance to the People."

The healer caught up with her young friend, who was dressed beautifully in tan leather embroidered with triangles of dyed porcupine quills. She wore high moccasins, not the low ordinary kind, and shells rattled at her ankles.

"You are dancing this year, I see."

"My family has always danced for Celebrations. This year my father has no wind for the dance, but I will follow his rhythm as he drums."

"You make a most beautiful dancer."

The two women walked slowly toward the house of Cricket Sings and her family.

"I am going to the practice, but I will return for your stories," said Soon to be Winter. Impulsively, she reached out to hug the old woman. "We are sisters both in our hearts and because we are the wives of brothers."

"That is true, wise woman. Your dream perplexed me, but I understand some of the mysteries. It is a very dark dream despite the light, and I think it foretells evil for the People. I have a strong sense that the future holds bad times. The evil journey may be your own or that of another, it is uncertain. Perhaps because this is a time of feasting the dream will soon be revealed. I think the masked man may be a Priest, but I cannot explain the blood about his mouth." She felt fear tighten in her chest as she remembered the stories about the Priests' taste for human flesh.

"Some of these thoughts had occurred to me," replied Soon to be Winter. "I fear not only for myself but also for the person who will live the reality of my dream." Her pretty face twisted. "I do not like such omens."

"We do not choose our fate, the Gods choose for us," admonished Cricket Sings. "Whether or not you like being a Seer, the Gods have decided you will be their instrument to reveal the future. You are a gift to your people. For some time I have considered taking an apprentice. Your special abilities would fit you for the role of healer. Would you be willing?"

"For my own part I would be most honored, but I must speak with my husband. I give much time to his stone work and he may not be able to spare me from those tasks."

The herb woman nodded in understanding. They had reached her house and she stopped at the door to watch the dancers walking down the road. Soon to be Winter continued on her way with a wave. The young woman was very tall and the power of her soul was reflected in her sure walk. Cricket Sings turned to enter the house.

CHAPTER FIVE
Priests

The clean bowls were stacked neatly in the corner and a cup of tea steamed on a rock next to the fire. Doe Eyes was gathering tidbits of dried meat, fish, and vegetables to make a nutritious soup for Wounded Deer. She put some tubers into the small brown bowl.

"Mother, it is nearly dark and I am going to Basket Maker's. The children are visiting Kills the Bear's new son with their father."

Doe Eyes walked to the door and lifted her long cloak from the peg where it had dried. She swirled it around in the air before settling it over her shoulders. Cricket Sings adjusted the mats, moving them here and there, bending over from the waist with her rump in the air because her knees were stiff. Finally, she sank back on her haunches in the corner and bowed her head to gather energy. Doe Eyes flipped the doorskin up over a peg so the dusk could enter to keep her mother company, then picked up the bowl and left to visit Wounded Deer.

Cricket Sings took three deep breaths and entered herself. She reached deep to that part of her ancestors which nestled within, finding spirits her grandmother had brought to the fireside. She began to rock and hum, matching the timing and tone of her song to the gathering rhythm of her thoughts. Searching among the many stories which flooded her mind, the old woman chose two of her favorites. Remembering the events of each tale, she pulled the stories about her like a warm robe and felt her face crease into a smile. When she opened her eyes, she was greeted by the smiles of People she loved. One by one the People had crept through the door, not even children making a sound. Now the house was full. Wolf Hunter was there with her grandchildren. Next to him sat Running Water, who had brought the two young brothers of her husband with her own family. At the far side of the fire, the length of two men away, was the shining face of Soon to be Winter. The dancer's eyes were bright with the excitement of learning new stories. There was a rustle at the doorway and Yellow Dog entered quietly, followed by his wife and the Basket Maker family. When they were seated next to One Eye and her orphans, Cricket Sings began the story.

"The brothers are Wind and Lightning, the sisters are Cloud and Rain. When they were of age, the Gods began the custom of marrying brother to sister, which continues among the People. When the Sun King marries his sister, she takes the name Moon.

"Sun and Moon talked with their children, pointing out the benefits of a good marriage, which are companionship, lovemaking, and children. Cloud and Rain were both enamoured of Lightning, for he was very sleek and beautiful. The sisters and Wind were jealous. Cloud knew that she was like Lightning, fancy and proud. Rain was shy, but there was much beauty hidden in her soft grey fall on the horizon.

"Lightning was a proud Warrior and knew the young ladies watched him walk across the sky. He made many dances, starting with a flash and low rumble and then flashing across the World with all his power. Wind was unhappy. He found the mysteries hidden in Cloud bewildering, but felt at home with the gentle Rain. He watched her secretly and knew he could sweep her across the sky. Lightning grew fearful of his pride. Rain wept in confusion.

"Sun and Moon decided to advise the Young Gods. They were wise children who valued the opinions and knowledge of elders. An understanding grew. Cloud looked at young Wind and decided he could not be her husband because she would never make a home for him. Instead, she chose the brighter and more fragile Lightning. Quiet Rain saw Wind anew and realized that he was a lover who could move her to span the World.

"So the marriages were made, brilliance to secrets and peace to wild howling. In honor of this great event, Sun taught the People magic and named them Priests. All were soon engaged in the duty of attending the Sun. There were no hunters and the People grew hungry. Finally the People came together and decided that the eldest son of the first man created would be the ruler. Sun asked the People to call this man the Sun King in his honor and gave him special magic. From that time forward our Sun King has been with us as the Sun in the World. We gather earth for holy hills to bring the Sun King closer to the great Sun in the Sky.

"Good hunters became Warriors by order of the First Sun King. He named as Honored Men those who make tools and carry on trade. Those who had no talents were named Ordinaries." The old woman paused a moment and thought of Little One, who would have remembered these stories for her own grandchildren. "The Gods and the People came together and were separated, as is the way of men and women. We are together for this time of Celebration to welcome a new year. The Priests have measured the travel of the Sun and in two days the sacred morning will grow bright."

She stopped and looked around for a moment before beginning the next story. The People she loved sat silently, waiting for her to begin.

"When the boy was born he had very long arms," she said. "Everyone knew that he would be a hunter, even though his father was a shell worker who made jewelry to adorn rich ladies. The father's eyes were not good, but he wanted his son to do what was right. When the boy learned to walk they went together to the edge of the river. There they saw the many fine willows which grow in wet places. 'This will make a perfect bow for you, my son,' the father said, as he cut a straight but slender willow with his knife. The father trimmed off the small branches, then bargained a shell brooch for a bit of deer sinew to make the bowstring. The boy's uncle was wise in the ways of hunting and made three small arrows, just the right size for a boy. His mother sewed a small quiver to hold the arrows. When the hunting kit was complete, the father placed a skin whitened with years of use on the ground against a tree. The boy aimed his arrows at this target, shouting with joy when he finally made a good hit.

" 'What is it? My son, why are you making so much noise?' the father would ask, squinting his poor eyes to see.

" 'Father, I have hit the target at last. It is true, I will be a hunter!'

"Long Arms became the best hunter of his people, but there was something missing from his life. It was not clothes, for his old mother did all his sewing. She cooked his food, and was a very good cook indeed. But on winter nights Long Arms wanted a wife and a house of his own, with children to roll about the campfire giggling. He wanted his old mother to tell stories to her grandchildren.

"Long Arms lived in a small village and there were very few eligible daughters nearby. He went first to the house of Grass in the Wind. She was a beautiful young woman and Long Arms laid a fine deerskin in front of her door. The next morning he found the very same skin lying at his own doorway. Grass in the Wind did not want him as her husband. There were two other unmarried maidens of the proper age in the village. One was very tall and thin. She had a sharp voice and was unkind. The second girl was short and fat with a cheery giggle, but she would not work hard because she was so fat. Long Arms could not make up his mind. He sat at the firesides of their fathers, but the cruel maiden kept making him move around and around the fire so she could sit out of the smoke. The other girl giggled inside the house and would not come out.

"In the spring a wise man came to town. The visitor was so old that his face was drawn into wrinkles you could not see between. His wife looked just like him, but even smaller and more bent. They were named Sun He Worships and Bright Moon. Well, the father and mother of Long Arms were very worried about their son. They did not know what to do. It was obvious that they needed a daughter-in-law. They invited the wise man and his wife, who was an herb woman, for soup and a bit of venison from a deer Long Arms had killed in the forest. When all their faces were shining with grease in the firelight, the father began to speak of the problem.

" 'You see, our son has no wife. We live in this village and it is so small that there are only three young women of the proper age nearby. One of them rejected our son, and it is just as well, for she is vain of her beauty. The other two girls are not worthy of him. The time for our grandchildren to come is passing.'

"Long Arms nodded sadly. He had wanted for many years to make a little bow for a son, as his father had done for him.

"The wrinkled man sat quietly, but the mother of Long Arms saw his wife poke him with her elbow. He shook his head slightly.

The wife bumped him with her elbow again and whispered into his ear. At last the old man nodded. He turned to Long Arms.

" 'You are a hunter of great power, I hear.'

"Long Arms swelled out his chest proudly and lifted up his head. 'Yes,' he said in a deep voice. 'It was known from my birth that I would be a hunter. I provide for my family and contribute food to the widows and old people who have no children.'

" 'I have a challenge for you,' the wise man said, and suddenly even the birds were quiet. 'If you accept this challenge and fulfill the promise, you will have a wife beautiful in both body and spirit. She is the perfect woman for you, Long Arms.'

"The young man pulled himself up proudly. 'Then I will take your challenge.'

" 'Go into the forest beyond the hills. In this place there will be many deer, but one is larger than all the rest. He has a red coat thicker and more beautiful than any you have ever seen. Bring me the skin of this buck and I will tell you where to find your bride.'

"Long Arms looked at his old mother, who was thin and sad because she had no babies to hold on her knee. Then he looked at his father, whose face had become lined with worry. The strangers waited patiently.

"Long Arms turned to the old couple who sat at his fireside with his parents. 'I will hunt this deer,' he said in a powerful voice.

"So Long Arms went off on a hunting trip over the far hills. He walked for many days with only a handful of berries and some dried fish to eat. He grew thin and weak, but saw no deer. Finally he could walk no farther and sat down under a tree to rest and plan the trip home. He fell into a heavy sleep and began to dream. His vision was a doe with fine ruddy fur, warm and thick on her body. She spoke to him with the voice of a young woman.

" 'Long Arms, you must rescue me from the evil magician who holds me in this form. There is a buck with antlers so wide you could hang robes on them and make a house. He put a spell on me and I cannot escape without your help. Please hurry, Long Arms!'

"The Warrior woke with a start. His body was stiff and cold. A snort and the rustle of last year's leaves came from the woods behind him. He turned to see a huge old buck with antlers larger than any he had known. The deer did not run away, but instead snorted again and pawed the ground as if to charge. The young hunter carefully drew an arrow from the quiver on his back and fitted it into his bow. He took aim and let the arrow fly. The buck fell heavily and Long Arms raced to cut its throat with his knife. With the blood staining his hands, he looked up to see the gentle doe of his dream stepping from the woods. Her eyes were large and deep, like pools of water in moonlight. The deer body faded until before him stood a beautiful young woman with long hair and large, gentle doe's eyes. She held out her hand.

" 'You have come to me, Long Arms, as my father said you would. I was captured by the evil spirit and now you have killed him and set me free.'

"Long Arms stared at her for only an instant before he jumped up and clasped her to him. 'You are the bride of my dreams, the woman I saw in my vision.'

"So the two, Doe Eyes and Long Arms, cooked some meat and ate of the flesh of their enemy. When their bodies were strong they carried the remainder of the magical food back to the village for their wedding feast. By the next spring their first son had been born and the old grandparents were happy at last."

Cricket Sings looked about her as though awakening from a trance. The fire had burned low and the People were huddled together, robes pulled close about their shoulders to keep out the night. A sleepy child murmured from the corner. Yellow Dog was first to rise. Unfolding his legs, he walked around the fire and held out his hand to Cricket Sings, who rested her hand in his for a moment. He turned and nodded to his wife as she rose to accompany him from the house. Wolf Hunter followed after the Basket Maker family to walk with them and escort his wife home. As the People left the house one by one, a young couple stopped to speak with Cricket Sings. Magic Fox stood before her with his beloved Praises Rain to ask a blessing for their marriage.

"You have discussed your likeness and differences?" the old woman asked shrewdly.

"We have done so," Praises Rain answered in a surprisingly deep voice. "We agree on where we will live and the ways we will teach our children."

"It is good to know, Magic Fox, that you have spoken with your lover as well as playing the flute behind trees."

Cricket Sings was relieved to see that the young man did not blush as he would have if his mind were not sure of this woman.

"She is the Moon to me," he said simply, holding out his hands, palms up.

"Because I attended at your births, I will speak with your mothers. I think they will agree with my suggestion that you are well suited to each other."

"Thank you, wise one," Praises Rain said softly.

"Good night, Honored Woman," added Magic Fox. "We will tell your stories to our grandchildren."

When the young couple left the house, Cricket Sings was alone except for her two grandchildren who slept like puppies in a heap of warm skins. From the edge of the pile the old woman selected three skins which were pliable and did not smell too bad. She unrolled her woven pallet and arranged two of the skins on top, throwing the other at one end to be used as a cover. Feeling the need to make water, she went into the damp night and hobbled to the toilet pit, relieved herself, and took the stick from a pile of dirt to knock some clods down into the pit as a covering. She returned to the house and drank a gourd dipper of water from the storage bottle near the door, then entered the house and sank onto her bed with a weary sigh, rolling onto her side to face the fire. With her mind absorbed in the patterns formed by the dusky red coals, the old woman fell asleep.

She woke before dawn. Grey light was slipping under the door-skin and there were rustling noises outside as though several people were moving about. Cricket Sings noted that her daughter and son-in-law were sleeping together on their side of the house, the children nestled near them. One set of footsteps became distinct in the damp grass and approached the door.

"Old woman," a hoarse voice whispered. "Old woman, we have need of medicine."

"I will be with you." She pushed back the warm robes and pulled on her dry overdress as protection from the lingering dampness. After combing and braiding her hair quickly, she stood to stretch before picking up the medicine bag and leaving the house. The sight of the visitors startled her and she stopped abruptly in the doorway.

Three Sun Priests stood with their backs to the door watching as the Sun signaled his imminent appearance with streamers of pink and gold across clouds left behind by yesterday's storm. Hearing the whisper of the doorskin, the tallest of the three turned and nodded regally.

"Who is the sick one?" the old woman asked in a calm voice, attempting to hide her surprise. Since the earliest times of the People a rivalry had existed between the Sun Priests and the herbalists. Priests depended upon the intervention of the Gods, while herbalists tried to find their cures in the World. The Priest did not answer, but shook his head back and forth.

"If you will not tell me the person's name, will you reveal the nature of the disease so that I may consider possible causes and cures?"

Again came the silent refusal. The tallest Priest indicated the road to the north by pointing in that direction. They began to walk toward the palisade gate, the tallest Priest in front and the others following behind. Before her, Cricket Sings saw a straight, brown back, adorned only by a sash embroidered in the most intricate patterns with beads of shell as well as brightly dyed quills. A skirt woven from plant fibers hung from a leather belt to the back of his knees. He wore silent boots, without the shell rattles which usually signaled the approach of a Priest. The hair was secured in a knot at the nape of his neck by two hairpins carved of finest tortoise shell. A leather thong was knotted around his neck. At the palisade gate the tall Priest turned toward her for a moment and Cricket Sings saw the copper rattlesnake ornament which swung from the thong.

The streets were silent and night still held the People in its hand of dreams. Two dogs rifled a garbage heap. Nearby, a hapless celebrant had fallen in a stupor against the wall of a house. Between the twin Hills of Death the old woman felt her usual ugly shudder. As they walked onto the plaza, she looked for her friend One Eye, but there was no sign of life among the green-flagged tents.

The Priest in front began to walk faster, moving diagonally across the plaza toward the Hill of the Sun King. Cricket Sings felt a thrill of fear. She had been careful not to reveal her dislike for the Priests to anyone she did not trust. With difficulty, she forced the rising terror back into her belly, hobbling faster to show the Priests that she understood the serious nature of this mission. The two younger Priests dropped behind as they approached the hill which held the house of the Sun King. When Cricket Sings turned the last corner before ascending the mound, they were no longer in sight. She felt evil behind her back and looked first over one shoulder, then the other. Nothing was visible, but the evil was there, waiting. It would only be harder to recognize.

The Priest turned and indicated that the herb woman was to follow him up the stairs to the top of the mound. She did not trust stairs and stepped slowly, lifting first one foot and then the other to each level. The terraces were uncomfortably wide for climbing and at the top her knees were trembling. She did not stop to consider whether the shaking was caused by exertion or fear, but instead followed the Priest toward the door of a large house. Sun was waking.

"Priest," she called out. "Let us linger a moment to worship the Sun."

He considered her request, the expression on his face betraying a conflict between his desires to hurry and to worship.

"Very well," he replied. "Keep your prayer time with the Sun."

He turned to face the growing light. Cricket Sings stood tall and began the low humming song with which she had comforted herself as a child. The same song had served as a lullaby for her own children. Now as her voice repeated the familiar syllables, strength grew in her belly. She followed the tempo of the wind and drew her song to a close just as Sun pulled his lower curve away from Night. For a moment she sank onto her knees with the fluid movements of a young woman. When she rose, her wrinkled self once more, she nodded serenely to the Priest, who had just finished his own worship. Turning back to the west, the old woman saw the glowing, sky-colored Father of Waters in the distance, the path which brought the People home. She walked toward the large house.

Behind a heavy doorskin the house was dark and filled with a strange sour scent from an herb Cricket Sings did not know. Acrid yellow smoke hung low. The fire in the center of the house was small, mostly glowing coals. On the far side of the room an old man rested on a pallet. He was surrounded by three Priests. The tall Priest motioned her toward the pallet and the others obligingly withdrew from the house. The old man's hair fanned out white and fine around his head. His eyes were closed and the breath came smoothly between his seamed lips. There was no other sound.

"What happened, and how long ago?" the herb woman asked.

The tall Priest answered in a peculiar whisper. "We were in the midst of a ceremony. He fell and has not regained his soul. We have prayed. The Sun Ceremony is approaching and if the old man cannot perform the Ceremony but still lives his son will not be able to take the role. We seek your counsel in this matter." He bowed briskly and without humility.

Cricket Sings was amazed. The old man on the pallet was the Sun King himself. She remembered the death of a Sun King in her youth, when she had escaped accompanying him into the Afterlife only because she was not perfect. Her twisted leg, source of so much pain and ridicule, had saved her life. Gathering courage, the old woman went to the pallet and gazed into the man's face. He appeared to be asleep, although his position was unnatural. Rather than taking the relaxed attitudes of slumber, he was stretched on his back with his legs extended and both arms straight against his sides. The same posture was used for the dead, and she shuddered involuntarily.

The young Priest was waiting silently on the far side of the fire. When she looked up his face was hidden and only the outline of his body could be seen through the swirling smoke.

"Has this man eaten mushrooms or herbs of a ceremonial nature?" she asked.

The smoke-shrouded figure remained perfectly still and a disembodied voice issued from the air. "We were engaged in a ceremony. He ate some seeds, but the Sun King has used seeds and mushrooms since childhood."

The old woman nodded and turned back to her patient. The seeds of the beautiful white-flowered god plant were poisonous when taken in large amounts and could be dangerous to a body weakened by age.

"How long?" she asked.

"Three days," the Priest replied. "Always before he has been strong within a day or two after the seeds."

"Have you attempted to wake him?"

"We have tried the most vigorous shaking and have applied heat and cold to his feet, but his soul remains hidden. You were suggested as one who has much knowledge of plants."

Cricket Sings sighed. She bent over the old man to smell his breath, which was warm and faint, slightly sour from the lack of moisture in his body. His skin felt dry as she took the hand nearest her own and squeezed it gently. There was no response. She pushed a sharp fingernail into his palm, but even the pain did not bring a flutter of his eyelids which might signal the return of his soul. She turned to the Priest.

"He has decided to die," she said.

The Priest nodded. "How much longer will he breathe? The Ceremony must be performed or the Sun will be displeased and the People may starve."

The old woman could see his jerky movements in the dim light and knew he must be worried.

"What will we do if the Sun King does not die so the Eagle may rise to his new role?" the young man asked.

She saw his body tighten and become calm. A deep assured voice replaced the hoarse whisper. "Wait here for Moon."

Cricket Sings was alone with the Sun King. She remained squatting at his side, although her legs were knotting with pain. She would not be guilty of disrespect.

Moccasined feet rustled at the door and Moon entered, followed by the same young Priest. Moon wore a fine pale robe trimmed in feathers and quills. A headdress of fur was woven into her long braids. Although her face was lined, Moon was not yet old.

"My husband is very ill, I understand," Moon said in a clear voice. She was the sister of the Sun King and had received a Priestly education.

"An evil spirit entered his body with the seeds," Cricket Sings replied. "A young man might have cast off the spell, but the Sun King is old and his body has begun to long for death. I think he will die soon."

"When?" Moon asked sharply, her pretty face freezing into a hard mask.

"I cannot say. He may live for a few days, no longer."

Moon nodded, then turned to the young man. Cricket Sings saw them exchange a powerful glance before they turned to her.

"Old woman," the Priest began in his new, deep voice. "We are in the midst of difficulty. Either the Sun King must die before tomorrow morning so that I may conduct the Sun Celebration or he must rise from his bed to perform the Ceremony himself. Unless we worship, our fields will be barren and the deer will run away. A night darker than any before will descend upon the People if we betray the Sun."

Cricket Sings knew what they wanted and she felt a sinking at her middle. Stimulating the old man to one last frenzy, or to death, were the two possible courses of action. Either way would be the end of him. If the Priesthood learned that she had poisoned the King, her whole family might be killed or banished. After a thick silence the herb woman spoke.

"I must consider our difficulty. I have not been asked to give death before, only life. Perhaps such a deed would not agree with my spirit. We do not have to decide until nightfall and it may be that he will die before then. I will return when the Sun is near night. Open the door and windows to let in light and air. Moisten his lips with water, but do not make him drink."

She rose to her feet and pulled down her overdress which had become wrinkled about her hips from sitting. Stooping to pick up her medicine bag from the floor, she gazed into the face of the Sun King for a long moment. None of the glory of Sun in the Sky was reflected in the worn face of this man. She hobbled to the door.

"Please send an escort to my house at late afternoon."

"No!" insisted the young Priest. "No one must know of the illness of the Sun King. If he dies on the eve of the Ceremony it will be a bad omen and must be kept secret. I will go forth to the Ceremony, but he must already be dead. Afterward we will announce that he was overcome during the Celebration following the Ceremony."

"A good idea," Moon agreed swiftly. "You will come here alone at the appointed time," she said, turning to the herb woman. "Pull a cloak over your face so you will not be recognized. Do as I say and do not tell anyone."

"Yes, Mother Moon," said Cricket Sings as she lifted the heavy doorskin and looped it over a peg at the top of the door. She stepped into morning. The scent of broken grass stems was welcome after the heavy atmosphere inside the house. She took a deep breath to clear both her body and spirit of the noxious herbs. The old woman slowly descended the side of the hill. Her sense of relief at leaving the house of death was overwhelming. The streets were filled with richly dressed People, hurrying on errands. No one noticed the old herb woman walking in an unsteady gait toward the plaza.

CHAPTER SIX
The
Black Bottle

Artisans had crowded into the City from towns and villages to sell the products of a year's work. Cricket Sings was drawn to a series of booths where shell traders displayed their wares. Shells from the far south glistened. The larger ones were suitable for use as spoons, and smaller shells had been drilled with sharp awls of flint and strung on sinews for necklaces. Round beads by the handful were strewn over the displays. She stopped to watch a young man drilling holes in tiny beads, a favorite purchase of mothers because such ornaments are most beautiful when strung about the plump brown neck of a baby. She kept a sharp eye out for clam shells, which made excellent hoes. The hoes of her family were chipped and worn. She saw two replacements.

"Merchant!" she called loudly.

The man turned, bent as though he were old, but his face was young. A gentle spirit was evident in his translucent gaze, and also in the fine quality of his work.

"I was looking at these hoes and wondering whether you might trade some shells for medicine to take on your travels. I know herbs which the People have used since the World began."

The young man hesitated a moment before answering. "I think we will be able to agree. I spend long seasons away from the City and might have need of medicines. An evil has taken root in my back and the pain is sometimes very bad."

Cricket Sings clicked her tongue in sympathy. "Once before I saw a young man whose back was stiffened and bent like yours. He was in much pain, and I recommended that he visit the sweathouse each morning. Heat decreases the pain. He also drank a decoction I made from the bark of the long-leaf tree. I happen to have some of this medicine with me and could instruct you in the recipe in return for these two hoe shells."

"That would be a good trade. I am Touch the Hawk. Have we met before?"

"I think not. Many People gather here for festivals, but I live in the City. My name is Cricket Sings." She reached into her medicine bag and rummaged until her fingers encountered the object. Her eyes opened wide and a smile creased her face as she pulled a packet from the bag. "Here is the long-leaf bark of which I spoke. It must be taken from the tree in spring, after the buds have swollen but before leaves appear."

"I know the time of year."

"This bark should be put into a large bowl of hot water. Set it in the Sun for a day, then near the fire to boil for another day. When the liquid is reduced by half and half again remove the bark. You may use it as a soothing poultice while it is hot. The most important part of the cure is to drink the liquid, a sip several times each day. This will help your pain."

"I thank you for the medicine. In return, please accept these two hoes. I have already cut holes for handles and you can bind them with sinew or plant fibers. I think they will serve well."

"Is your wife with child? I would trade a good birthing medicine for some of these tiny shells. I have two grandchildren who would look very fine with such shells about their necks."

"Honored Woman, I have no wife as yet, although I have been looking for a woman to share my life. Please, accept these beads in return for medicine at some time in the future." He pushed a few beads toward her.

The old woman thought for a moment. "No," she said. "I will not accept the beads now, but I have two young nieces who may be looking for husbands. Perhaps you would like to come to my house tonight? I am telling stories around the fire."

"Yes, I would like to hear your stories."

"Good! Go south on the road from the palisade gate and when you come to the two burial mounds between the lakes ask anyone where Cricket Sings lives. They will take you to my house. Come at dusk; my nieces will be there."

"I will see you at dusk, old one."

"At dusk," she repeated as she turned away. The plaza was crowded with buyers and sellers now. In the central area the men were playing their games. Cricket Sings noticed the well-muscled beauty of their bodies. Two men were making a bet. A tall Warrior threw out a fine bear skin, rare in the City. The second man laid a spear trimmed with feathers on top of the skin. The game began and she stopped to watch. The first man picked up a smooth discoidal stone and walked to the starting point of the game field. The second man joined him. Each held a spear in one hand. The first man skillfully rolled the stone down a dirt path in the center of the field. As soon as the stone left his hand both men ran after it, trying to guess where the stone would stop. The second man gave a high-pitched shout and threw his spear in front of the rolling stone. The other man then launched his own spear toward a point a little farther down the field. They ran anxiously to see who would win the bearskin and spear. Cricket Sings stood on her toes to watch. A shout went up from the crowd and the second man cheered excitedly. The chunky stone had toppled to the ground touching his spear. He leapt into the air and howled, his face contorted with glee. The first man shrugged nonchalantly to hide his disappointment and waved at the old woman, who recognized him as a younger brother of Kills the Bear.

Cricket Sings turned away with a wave. She always liked the winners and felt sorry for the losers. She thought of her first husband, Smells Like A Fish, a gambler who had lost his hunting equipment and all their warm robes. She had begged him to stay home from the games, but Smells Like A Fish had been determined to win. Returning home a loser once more, he found his moccasins where she had placed them outside the door. She smiled to think of her younger self gathering the strength to end the marriage.

Ahead were the herb sellers and she quickened her pace with excitement. One Eye was sitting in the same place as yesterday, her seamed face turned up to the warmth of Sun. Behind her, two young women were grinding herbs in the shade of a skin awning.

"Hello, old one," Cricket Sings called. "I am in need of wise counsel today."

One Eye turned her sightless face toward the sound of her friend's voice. Her toothless gums gleamed pink and new in her old face as she smiled.

"Welcome once more," she said, patting the ground at her side. "Sit and talk with me."

Cricket Sings skirted three Warriors hurrying toward the chunky games and approached the older woman. Shrugging her bag off her shoulder, she set it down carefully, then plopped to the ground in a most undignified manner.

"I am so glad you are here," she said in a low voice. "I have a problem and you are the only person I trust to help me. Your wisdom is needed."

One Eye nodded. "It is always better to have the opinion of elders you trust."

"I have been to the house of the Sun King. He has eaten the seeds with which Priests induce holy frenzies. When his visions ended he fell into sleep and has not awakened. Moon and the heir Eagle are afraid of what may happen if the Sun King is unable to perform the Ceremony in the morning. They asked me to give the old man medicine so that he may do the holy things once more or to kill him so that Eagle may assume the role of Sun King. Either action could have grave consequences for my family."

One Eye's mouth wrinkled into an O. She did not speak, but her hands were tightly clenched in her lap. Under her breath, One Eye began to hum her mourning song. Cricket Sings watched her friend, knowing that the other woman might not help with such a difficult problem. She spoke softly once more.

"I must decide what to do. If I refuse to kill the Sun King and he does not die, the Sun will be displeased and the People may perish. But in the past those who have tried to injure the Sun King or his family have been taken to the High Hill never to be seen again. The risk is very great." Cricket Sings began to hum her own mourning song.

Suddenly, One Eye broke off her song. "You have done much good healing for the People. If the Sun King does not die, you can hide your knowledge of his illness and let the heir perform the Ceremony. This blasphemy would keep the People from fear. Your other choice is to help the Sun King die. There is a liquid which I have kept for many years. A few drops bring death in a short time, but if you take this course you may be choosing the death of your family if anyone learns of your treason."

"Whatever I do will be treason, yet by the laws of the People I cannot refrain from action."

"Can you trust Moon and Eagle?"

"I do not know. The gossip of the City says they are good."

One Eye nodded again, mixing this information with her own knowledge of human nature. "I think their interest is to see that Eagle becomes the new Sun King. You must also consider the possibility of an upset of the holy family. Perhaps one of the uncles will try to assume the place of the rightful heir. If that happens, your own treason could be exposed. However, if you can hide your actions and the family is loyal you may live safely through this difficulty."

"You will give me the poison?"

"Yes, if you will say you have kept it in your bag for many years in case of need. Who is to know that it was in my bag instead?"

"This I will do."

"Daughter," One Eye called loudly. "Daughter, bring my bag. I wish to make my friend Cricket Sings a present of some tea."

The taller of the two young women brought the medicine bag of One Eye, which was patched in several places. The old woman ran her hand over the side of the bag until she came to the quilling around the drawstring opening. She sensed that her daughter was still standing nearby and spoke sharply.

"Back to work, lazy one. We must trade or the winter will be hungry. Already I have felt a cold wind in my bones."

The young woman turned silently and walked back to join her sister.

"That one had her tongue cut out for lying," explained One Eye. "I found her in the road, nearly dead. She has been faithful to me ever since."

When she no longer heard her daughter's footsteps, One Eye pulled on the drawstring and opened her bag. She removed a tiny pottery bottle stoppered with a piece of wood carved in the shape of a bird's head. The bottle was black and looked evil. She spoke in a low voice.

"This is the potion. A few drops on the tongue will produce painless death. It was given to me by my grandmother. I have never used such potions, but I saved this one for relief from the pain of evils that kill slowly. Perhaps for myself."

"I have sometimes wished for a medicine to end the pain of such evils," Cricket Sings said. "Yet the wisdom of the People says we are born in pain and must die in pain."

One Eye removed a small piece of skin tied with a thong and a chunk of bark from her bag. She held both objects in her hand, placing the small black bottle between them so that it was hidden should anyone be watching their conversation.

"Here are some teas," she said in a loud voice. "Which I gathered in years past and have no use for now."

Cricket Sings placed her hands around One Eye's and transferred the three objects to her lap. She reached for her own bag and slipped the three packages inside, then gave a small sigh of relief. "We are done with it, One Eye," she whispered. "I thank you, old one. Your teas have warmed many winters." She hesitated. "There is something else . . ." she began, then stopped suddenly without finishing. Her stomach was growling fiercely in response to the good smells drifting downwind from the stalls of the foodsellers. "My hunger is talking," she said with a smile. "My daughter promised fresh corn bread and I must return home. We will talk of this other matter later. Will you come to my story tonight?"

"You know that I would not miss your stories unless I were dead."

"At dark, then, old one." Cricket Sings stood, rocking back and forth to loosen the tightness which grew in her knees when she remained in one position for a long time. She touched her friend's shoulder to let her know that she was leaving, then grabbed the strap hanging from her bag and pushed through the crowd on the road, ignoring the good odors as she passed the stands of the food sellers. She looked for dancers, but saw none. The dances would not start until Sun had begun his descent toward Night. The plaza was crowded with both City-dwellers and those who had come from the surrounding countryside. It was truly a gathering of the People, and excitement came as much from seeing old friends as from the ceremonies. As she neared the palisade, the old woman saw Yellow Dog. A thought to tell him of the morning's events leaped through her, but she knew he had taken on many Northern ways and might not understand. Instead, she greeted him with a wave and a broad smile.

"Hello cousin! We have a good day for dancing and feasting."

"Yes, and also for trading. I have supplied many friends with copper this year and in return I have received pottery and fine shell jewelry which is difficult to obtain in the North City. Where are you going?"

"I am on my way home. Running Water has prepared a feast which we will eat after the Ceremony tomorrow morning. We will eat all day and into the night until our bellies are round enough to play like drums. You and your family are most welcome to feast with us."

"I spoke with Running Water this morning. She wanted to trade for a copper ornament to hang around her husband's neck."

Cricket Sings giggled. "Yes, my sister has a weakness for men with powerful necks. I have seen her watching the dancers with a lust unseemly in a woman her age."

"Old woman, there is nothing unseemly about lust. It is the sinew which binds men and women together," Yellow Dog chided.

"You are right." She thought for a moment of Sand Crane, but then her stomach began to growl insistently. "I am very hungry, it is time to go. Please come to my house tonight. At dusk I will tell a story I learned from our grandmother."

"We will certainly attend. Fill your belly well, old woman."

Yellow Dog strode off toward the center of the plaza, his bundle of trade goods held securely in the crook of his left arm. Cricket Sings looked after him for a moment, then turned toward the palisade and her home. She passed the house of Running Water on the way, and stopped when she smelled the roasting venison. Her stomach growled again. Two great haunches of meat hung suspended over the fire. Talking Tree, the young daughter, was turning the meat as it browned. As the herb woman approached, her short-sighted niece gasped in surprise.

"Oh, Aunt, I had no idea you were there. I will call Mother."

The girl rose and hurried into the house. Running Water pushed the doorskin aside and stuck her head out.

"Hello, my sister, you are here to visit and this is most delightful. Preparations for the feast are going well; by tomorrow everything will be ready. Did I ask you to bring some yellow flower tea and perhaps a few corn breads?" The plump woman walked out of the house toward her elder sister. "Of course, I asked you yesterday and you said you would. Yellow Dog is bringing his family; it will be strange to meet his wife. I hear Northern women are peculiar, that is what my neighbor says, although she has never met one. Would you like to taste the meat? My husband Starving Creek killed this buck himself and it was young and fat."

Running Water did not pause in her speech as she pulled a stone knife from the pouch hanging at her waist and cut a small piece of meat from the larger of the two haunches. She pulled at the meat to divide it into halves, handing one to Cricket Sings and chewing on the other herself. The herb woman took advantage of the sudden silence provided by her sister's full mouth.

"We will be attending your feast tomorrow and bringing both tea and corn breads. Who would miss such an event when the food is being prepared by the best cook in the City?" She took a bite of the meat and closed her eyes at the juicy taste. "It is very tender, just as your husband promised."

"Yes, you are right," replied Running Water through a full mouth. "I have collected roots and we will make a good vegetable broth. Everyone will bring corn breads and drinks. I certainly hope Rain will stay away from the Ceremony and our feast. It will be most uncomfortable if we have to crowd into the house. People need room to lie down and relax after a fine meal. Sister, do not forget to bring bowls for your family because I will not have enough. Bowls are expensive this year. I had to trade three baskets of corn to replace the large water jug my clumsy daughters broke." Running Water sat down on a mat near the fire and Cricket Sings squatted beside her.

"I stopped to tell you that my story will not begin until dark tonight. At dusk I must see one who is very ill. If I am not home when you arrive, help yourself to corn bread and see that my guests are comfortable. I have invited a young man. You have two marriageable daughters and he is one who would not take away your wealth. Tell my nieces to dress well. Perhaps they should visit the sweathouse, men always like a clean woman."

"You are right sister, I would like to have these daughters married. They clutter my house with their moccasins. Who is this young man?"

"A shell trader, good and honest although he has an evil in his back which bends him like a bow. He is otherwise handsome and of gentle demeanor and would make a good son-in-law."

"I have been looking among the Warriors, but no husbands have appeared. Starving Creek spoke to his friends, but they do not want even rich wives. Have you eaten enough, or would you like another tidbit? You would, I can tell. Come here, sister, this haunch is not carefully balanced." As she spoke, Running Water stood and steadied the meat suspended on a strong tree limb over the fire. "This is going to be a most pleasurable Ceremony, I can see already that the costumes are beautiful. There are more People in the City than I remember in any year."

Cricket Sings stepped forward to help hold the meat so it would not fall into the fire. Running Water cut a thick, crisp slice. Suddenly the herb woman thought of the man lying silently on his pallet at the top of the hill.

"I must go," she said abruptly and turned toward her house. Running Water, used to her sister's ways, was not alarmed by her behavior. She continued to hack at the meat. Cricket Sings walked very fast. The smoke was rising from the roof hole, perhaps Doe Eyes was inside. As she came closer to the house the old woman saw the new mats promised by Yellow Dog hanging in the windows and door of the house. They looked light and airy. Doe Eyes emerged from the house, carrying Son. Little Daughter was clinging to her skirt.

"Hello, Mother," she called. "I missed you. We are going to the sweat house to bathe, would you like to come along?"

"I am very hungry. If I could have a bit of porridge or a corn bread I would accompany you afterward."

"Poor Mother, hurrying off with no food to keep your old legs from wobbling. Sit by the fire and I will fetch a bit of bread I saved just for you."

The old woman nodded and sat down on her mat. Doe Eyes placed Son in his cradleboard and tied him securely before leaning the board against the house near his grandmother. Daughter ran and climbed into Cricket Sings' lap, chattering in her strange baby language.

"Sometimes I think you are from the North City," the old woman teased. "When will you learn the language of the People?"

"Sing!" the little girl said distinctly and patted her grandmother on the arm. "Sing!"

"Yes," answered the delighted old woman. "I am Cricket Sings and because this is your first word perhaps you will have a name which sings when you are older."

She gathered her granddaughter to her flat bosom and rocked the giggling child. Daughter wiggled free and ran to her mother as Doe Eyes came out of the house with the bread.

"Sing!" The little girl pointed to the old woman at the fireside. Her eyes were sparkling in her chubby face.

"Why yes, Daughter, that is your grandmother, Cricket Sings. What a good girl you are." Doe Eyes bent to hug the child before handing the corn bread to her mother.

Cricket Sings ate as though she had been through a starving winter. In a few moments only crumbs remained. She sighed and patted her belly. "It is a wonder that I am not a fat woman the way I like to eat."

"You are too busy to grow fat, Mother. Only lazy women have time to eat so much."

Doe Eyes picked up Son and clucked her tongue at Daughter, who was wandering toward the neighbor's house. The old woman stood slowly, patted her belly again, then picked up her bag and placed it carefully inside the house. She thought of the black bottle inside and for the first time felt that her bag was unsafe. She moved the bag to the back of the house, piling skins on top, then looked to see whether her daughter had noticed this behavior. Doe Eyes was already walking down the road toward the bathing area. Cricket Sings flipped the new mat carefully down over the doorway and hurried to catch up.

CHAPTER SEVEN
An Omen

The two women walked along the curve of the lake. Ahead the sweathouse was smoking and they could hear the delighted screams of children playing in the water nearby. Next to the road laborers walked in lines carrying baskets of earth to build a new holy hill. Cricket Sings saw Carries Stones and waved. The Ordinary was followed by his two older children, but Little One had not yet resumed her place in line.

"Mother," said Doe Eyes, "Where were you this morning? I did not hear you rise and there was no sign to tell me where you had gone."

"I was called to see a most important person and could not wait to leave you a sign. At dusk I will return to check on the progress of this man."

"He must be of high rank if you are not able to tell me," the younger woman probed.

"I do not like guessing games, daughter. Here is the sweat house. I am going to get warm so my old bones will be limber. Will you bring the children inside?

"Just for a short while. If they become too hot we will leave and play in the lake."

Cricket Sings began to shed her clothes, piling them neatly at the side of the sweathouse. Although she washed daily and often bathed in the lake, the sweathouse was a special treat which made her feel clean and new from the inside. The sweathouse was built like any other house, but the thatch was tightly woven without windows, only a smoke hole at the very top. Inside, coals were heaped around hot stones in the firepit. Doe Eyes stripped her children, folding their garments. After removing her own clothes, she walked to the shore of the lake and washed her son's buttocks, then splashed water toward Daughter, who giggled and tried to splash back.

"I am ready," the old woman called.

Doe Eyes turned to enter the sweathouse with her mother. As they pulled back the thick doorskin, a cloud of hot air escaped, rich with the smell of many bodies. They entered and found seats along the wall near the door. Coals in the fireplace gave off a dim red glow.

"This feels so good, I would like to sweat every day," Doe Eyes whispered.

"A sweatbath is good from time to time, but to do this every day might take some of the spirit from your body. You would be weak. If your bones are sore, however, the sweathouse is the best medicine."

The women relaxed among friends and neighbors, stretching out their legs and gossiping in the heat. Kills the Bear's new Warrior had been seen by nearly everyone and they all agreed that the child would be a powerful hunter. Son sat on Doe Eyes' lap and Daughter squirmed into position between her mother and grandmother. The sweat gathered in beads at the back of their necks and began to run from their foreheads into their eyes. A woman on the far side of the fire rose and left the sweathouse. Cricket Sings felt her knees loosen. She bent and extended her legs several times, enjoying the freedom of movement. Doe Eyes touched her mother's arm and spoke quietly.

"My son is too warm. I should take him outside."

The baby's cheeks were very red.

"Take Daughter also," the old woman urged. "I will be along shortly."

Doe Eyes stood and lifted Son onto her hip. She took Daughter by the hand and pushed aside the heavy doorskin with her shoulder. Cricket Sings felt very hot, but stayed in the sweathouse until she was completely clean. When she rose, she bowed to the women in the sweathouse before leaving. The Sun was very bright and the old woman squinted.

"Phew," she said, wiping her forehead with the back of one hand. "It certainly is hot in there. Hand me that shell, Doe Eyes, and I will finish cleaning myself."

Doe Eyes gave her mother a flat clamshell used to scrape sweat from the skin and walked to the edge of the lake, then stood ankle deep in the cool water, looking out to the trees at the far side. Little Son was sitting in the shallow water, patting at the strange liquid with fat hands. Daughter was laughing and splashing as she crawled on her belly.

Doe Eyes bent to catch Son as he tipped over on his side and splashed water on him gently to remove any sweat she had not been able to scrape off. Balancing the baby once more in a sitting position, Doe Eyes sat beside him and began to splash her own body with water. Cricket Sings joined her. When the women were cool, they stood and walked to their clothes, Doe Eyes carrying the baby. Daughter continued to play in the lake.

"Are you going to the dances this afternoon, Mother?" Doe Eyes pulled her dress over her head.

"Yes, I think so, but I must see my friend Little One, the child with the burned foot."

"I remember her well. Each time I pass her house on the way to the fields she calls out to me from her place beside the fire. A child that age should be running and playing."

"Little One does not think of how soon she will play, but rather of how she can help her father carry dirt to bring the Sun King and the Priests closer to the skies and thus obtain a larger ration of corn for her family."

"Mother, children that small should not be forced to work, even in the service of the Sun!"

"We both know that is true, but a hungry child thinks of food, not play. I have had some thoughts about the little girl which perhaps you should share. You know that for some time I have been looking for an apprentice."

Doe Eyes nodded and Cricket Sings sat down to put on her moccasins, brushing dirt and small pebbles off the soles of her feet. The old woman continued.

"Well, I have two in mind, the Little One and Soon to be Winter."

Doe Eyes had begun lacing Son into his cradleboard. She looked up. "Mother, I think Soon to be Winter is a Seer more than a healer. That is not to say that she cannot become a good herb woman, but rather that her calling may be elsewhere. Little One has much acquaintance with pain and healing. If she can remember the recipes, she may make a good apprentice."

"You have echoed my own thoughts. I would like to protect Soon to be Winter from the power of her visions, but that may be impossible."

Doe Eyes finished dressing Son and captured the small wiggling body of Daughter, who was delighted with this game and attempted to run away. Finally, Doe Eyes gave up and returned to Son, lifting the cradleboard onto her back for the trip home. Daughter ran naked through the tall grass as the women walked slowly down the road.

"I must visit Little One," Cricket Sings said again. "She does not need my care, but the child has grown to depend on me. Perhaps if her mother is home we will discuss the possibility of the child being apprenticed to me."

"You will probably have to buy Little One. Her family must think you are rich."

"I am wealthy in comparison to Ordinaries."

Doe Eyes left her mother at the path to their house. "I will see you later, old woman. Stop on your way back and we will walk to see the dancers. Wolf Hunter has gone to the hills with his brothers to hunt."

"A good thing, for although he is not a gambling man, the chunky games are difficult for a Warrior to resist."

Doe Eyes waved and turned away. As Cricket Sings walked the familiar road toward the edge of the City, she rehearsed the speech she would give the mother of Little One. They would have to find a new name for the girl, a pretty name. At the house of Crow Eater and Soon to be Winter the old woman hesitated, but only a thin stream of smoke rose from the fire. The couple had left early, probably to join the dancers who were preparing their contribution to the ceremony. When Cricket Sings reached the houses of the Ordinaries, she would see a small figure waiting by the fire of Carries Stones. Today the child was not alone; her mother was bent over the grinder. Walking closer, the old woman heard the two singing the grinding song of the People.

> A good woman
> grinds the corn
> for a whole morning.
> Her bread is firm and flat
> crisp, but not harsh to the tooth.

They looked up as she approached.

"Good day, Honored One," said the mother, whose name Cricket Sings never could remember.

"Hello, mother, and how is our Little One today?"

"I am very well, Cricket Sings," piped the child. "My foot is much better and I have walked to the woodpile and back two times."

"That is wonderful!" exclaimed the medicine woman, although she was not surprised. The time was right for the child to begin walking.

Little One unwrapped her foot to show the healing and the two women drew close to watch. Cricket Sings rubbed the foot with bear grease ointment, kept by the mother in her best pot, and rewrapped it.

She turned to the other woman. "Mother, I would like to talk with you about your daughter. For some time I have been in need of an apprentice, but no one of talent has appeared. A healer must have a good memory for recipes, as well as an understanding of pain so she will not cause undue harm. You child has both. I would like Little One to be my apprentice until she is able to conduct treatments of her own. She would have status as an Honored Woman and would not have to depend on a husband for her living."

The mother's eyes darkened at the thought of her daughter becoming a member of the Honored. She considered for only a moment. "Yes," she said firmly. "My child will have food and useful work. I hate to see my sons carrying dirt from the pits day after day in return for a ration of corn which will never make them fat. Please, take her." The woman pushed Little One toward Cricket Sings.

"The child will be like my own daughter," promised the herb woman. "Perhaps you will accept a small payment of some warm robes or corn in return for loss of the child's help."

"Corn would be most welcome to help feed the two boys. Daily they grow thinner from their labors."

"It is done, then. My son-in-law Wolf Hunter will come to get the child. She should not walk until her foot is healed completely."

During the conversation Little One had remained silent. The old woman turned to her.

"Is this apprenticeship your own will?" she asked gently, bending toward the child until their eyes met.

Little One did not speak, but nodded her head vigorously up and down. Cricket Sings nodded in return.

"Wolf Hunter will carry you to my house. You will hear my stories around the fire. Until then, may Sun bless you."

"And yourself," the mother answered.

Cricket Sings walked between the huts of the Ordinaries toward the road. She noticed garbage piled up outside the houses and knew it was time for the Honored and Warriors to make the Ordinaries dig pits and bury their refuse. The upper classes were careful to keep rubbish at a minimum so disease would not clench the City in an ugly fist. Ordinaries did not care if they walked in garbage, so Warriors marched through the streets several times each year to make the residents clean up their trash.

When Cricket Sings reached the house of the Basket Maker family, young Wounded Deer was lying on a pallet near the fire, watching his mother, aunt and uncle working nearby. The aunt and uncle were weaving the great round baskets used for corn storage and Shade of the Tree was grinding corn for breads.

"Hello," the herb woman called. "How is the young Warrior today?"

"Much recovered," answered the mother, her pretty face dimpling into a smile. "Here is the young man himself, enjoying the Sun. I think he will be well enough to attend the Ceremony if his father carries him."

The boy grinned and lifted himself onto his elbows so he was almost sitting. "See how strong I am?" he asked.

"Indeed you are a powerful young man. Have you eaten?" questioned the old woman.

"My cousin Doe Eyes brought me some meat and mother made broth with roots and berries. I ate a whole bowl this morning."

"You should eat more of such good soup and also chew on the meat. Have you need of medicine?"

The mother answered. "I think not, Honored Woman. The boy eats well and drinks a cool tea made from roots of the north."

"Good! If his pain returns we will give more medicine. I promised Doe Eyes I would walk to the dances with her, so I must hurry. The story will not begin until dark tonight. Will you join us?"

"Of course," answered Shade of the Tree, bending her head slightly to the old woman. "How else am I to know the stories of my son's father?"

Cricket Sings left the Basket Maker family to their labor. She walked toward her own house, enjoying the sight of so many strong People. The street was crowded, but no dancers were visible. They were probably all at the plaza, she thought as she waved at a neighbor. She remembered birthing a young mother who was now walking in the road with two children of her own and passed a tall thin man she had cured of a strange evil which caused sores to spread all over his body. Doe Eyes was sitting in front of the house, tapping her fingers on the cradleboard.

"Mother, I thought you would never get here. I like the dancing so much and now if we don't hurry we will miss it. Can you take Daughter by the hand? I will carry Son." Doe Eyes stood and swung the cradleboard onto her back, balancing it with the strap which lay across her forehead.

"I have been slow today, daughter, but I did not mean to keep you waiting. The arrangements with Little One's mother are finished. We will go to the dances; I have a few medicines we can trade for a corn bread or two."

The old woman hurried into the house to retrieve her medicine bag. Doe Eyes peered curiously after her as she rummaged through the pile of skins.

"Mother, why did you hide your bag?"

Cricket Sings was startled at her daughter's words. Guilt flashed through her body. "Ah . . . Ah, I thought with so many People here from the country, it might be safer." The old woman fumbled for words. "Never mind, child," she commanded suddenly, her head lifting to a proud angle. "My reasons are my own and you should not question those older and wiser."

"You are older and wiser, it is true, but you are also deeply loved by your family and when you have secrets I worry."

"Well, you will have to worry for a long time before you learn this one!"

Grabbing her bag roughly, the old woman left the house and hobbled down the road as fast as she could. Little Daughter ran after her, calling out in baby language. The old woman stopped and took the child by the hand, then turned her back on Doe Eyes. As they passed Running Water's house, the younger woman caught up.

"Mother," she said, panting. "I am sorry for questioning you. It was out of love, not disobedience. Should we stop and ask my aunt to walk with us to the plaza?"

"I think they have already left. See, the meat is hidden in the tree so the dogs cannot reach it."

"Ah, I see, there it is. Perhaps we will see them at the dances. I am so excited, I have always wanted to be a dancer. Listen, I hear drums now."

Cricket Sings tilted her head so her ears would catch the sound. In the distance, the high rhythm of skin drums was complemented by the deeper rumbling water drums. Hollow stumps were filled with water and a membrane was stretched over the open mouth, giving out a growling sound when rubbed with a stick. The drums called the People from their homes and they suddenly crowded into the street leading toward the narrow palisade gate, waiting to enter the central City. Cricket Sings lifted Daughter and cradled the child in her arms. As they passed through the gate, Doe Eyes saw Running Water, Starving Creek, and their daughters ahead. They were talking with a dancer painted in black and white stripes. His hair stood up in a stiff fringe around his head. As he turned the black and white feathers on his breechcloth rustled. About his ankles strings of shells rattled and clicked. He was ready, moving from foot to foot in time with the rhythm of the drums.

"Running Water," the herb woman shouted. "Sister, here we are."

Running Water turned and waved. "We are talking to this most interesting man who has come from the South to dance for our

Celebration," she shouted. "It is wonderful to have other dancers here besides our own. Isn't his costume frightening? Do you think he will scare away spirits which might harm our Ceremony?"

"We are going to see the dance. Perhaps you would like to walk with us?" Cricket Sings asked.

Stepping in front of his wife, Starving Creek cut her off before she could begin another waterfall of words. "Yes, we will walk quietly behind you and listen to the music." He gave Running Water a stern look.

The family moved toward the plaza. As Cricket Sings passed between the death hills, she ignored her shivering response, but could not stop the pictures of the Sun King lying in his last sleep from entering her mind. The time was not ready and she put her worries behind her.

The afternoon was warm and beautiful. Fluffy white clouds augered well for continued sunshine. The sky was deep and Sun was fierce, although a breeze gentled his heat. Cricket Sings pushed ahead through the crowd, followed by Doe Eyes and the family of Running Water.

The dance had just begun and men moved slowly toward the center of an open area. The chunky players had been temporarily displaced and stood, disgruntled but interested, in a group at the north end of the plaza. The drummers quickened their rhythm from Calling the People to The First Dance. With fine gestures and whirling movements meant to beguile and capture the Sun, the men wove their lines. They were accompanied by high ringing drums rather than the rumbling water drums. The rhythm was steady and soon a hush crept over the crowd as they began to move in time with the dance, joining in with their bodies as well as their spirits. Cricket Sings swayed, transferring her weight from one foot to the other. Daughter felt the movement and began to lean back and forth with her grandmother. The crowd became One and the special feeling of the People for their kind rose in each heart. Cricket Sings began to hum the Song and the humming spread outward through the crowd.

The timbre of the drums changed and a deeper note crept in. A line of young women stepped gracefully into the plaza and the men faded back into the crowd. Although the costumes made recognition difficult, Cricket Sings thought she could see Soon to be Winter in the first row. The young Seer had a particular air of pride about her dancing which was evident even at a distance. The women danced with an ear of last year's corn in each hand, for after the Sun has been called the corn must grow for the People to live. The young women bowed before the Sun and their beauty was hypnotic. Suddenly, with a wild screech, youths ran into the plaza like Rain, scattering the corn before them. The corn rows re-formed and danced through the Rain and the rhythm quickened. Finally, the young corn women stretched their arms to the sky to simulate growth. When the drums stopped, the assembled People continued their low humming for a time, then gradually they began to disband. A few wandered off to gamble or trade, but many stayed to talk with friends and family, enjoying the sense of One-ness that engulfed the People after dances. Foreigners began to demonstrate the steps of their lands. Cricket Sings turned away; it was nearly dusk.

"I have a sick man to see," she murmured, handing Daughter to Doe Eyes. "Can you take the children home by yourself? Let's ask Night Bird and Talking Tree to walk home with you and help keep Daughter within arm's reach."

"A good . . ."

Doe Eyes was interrupted by screams from the front of the crowd. The voice changed to a terrified wailing. Something horri-ble had happened. Cricket Sings pushed her way through the Peo-ple toward the sound. She saw a young woman screaming and clutching a bloody cradleboard. Apparently the mother had grown tired of holding her baby and had set the cradleboard at her feet, leaning against a tree. One of the hungry dogs which continually skulked at the edge of the People had come upon the child while the mother was preoccupied with the dance.

Cricket Sings saw at once that there was nothing she could do. Too much of the child's head was missing for it to be alive. This was a fearful omen. She turned her attention to the mother, who was screaming and choking on her tears. The old woman grabbed the girl by the shoulders and shook her once, then again.

"Stop it, Mother!" said the herb woman harshly under her breath. "I know you grieve for your child, but this omen must not spread further through the crowd."

The mother understood and quieted her wailing to hiccoughs. She moaned as though the wounds were her own. A tall young man stepped out of the crowd and put his arm around her.

"I am her brother," he said. "I will take her home so the Celebration may continue unshadowed."

He took the bloody cradleboard from his sister's arms and handed it to a companion, then walked the sobbing woman through the crowd, which parted in a wide arc leading to the gate. The friend followed with his burden. A Warrior had caught the dog and now he lifted the animal by the neck and strangled it swiftly, throwing the limp body down next to the tree. The dog's muzzle was covered with blood.

Feeling the dark spirits press in around her, Cricket Sings turned back to her own family, but they had taken the opportunity to slip away. She walked toward the herb sellers on the plaza, looking for One Eye. When she reached the green-flagged stall, One Eye was not there, nor were any of her children. Cricket Sings shook her head in despair. These burdens were too much for one woman. She suddenly doubted her own ability to overcome the lurking evil. The afternoon was growing late. Already Sun had passed into the western sky. The rim was very close to Night and the old woman knew she must hurry.

The People had dispersed; the last few were walking toward their homes and campsites. Around the limp body of the dog a small crowd remained, whispering of witchcraft and half-remembered evils. Across the Plaza, Priests were preparing for the Ceremony. A fat man fluffed the feathers of a long cape which hung before his house, the color and size of the cape showing the owner's importance to the Gods. Lesser Priests had short capes in dark colors, while those higher in station had longer, more brilliantly colored capes. The Sun King himself would wear yellow feathers which swept the ground.

Cricket Sings wove through the narrow streets surrounding the base of the holy dwelling mound. She noticed that no fires were smoking in the houses of the Priests, although the rest of the City was filled with the odors of roasting dog and venison. Perhaps they would have their feast on the Holy Hill, she thought. As she reached the stairway leading to the Sun King's house, the herb woman was joined by two silent Priests, who took up a position behind and a little to each side, following her slow pace as she climbed the stairs. A silence hung in the air, so thick that Cricket Sings felt she had to push it aside to approach the house.

CHAPTER EIGHT
The Sun King

The silence was broken by a loud whisper. "Wait! Old woman, I say wait!" Panting, the shorter of the two Priests caught up. "The Sun King has been moved to the Holy Hill. We will be your escort; you would not be allowed to ascend alone."

The man turned abruptly and began marching toward the far side of the dwelling hill. Cricket Sings followed without a word as he led the way across to stairs which descended the north side. The second Priest fell into step behind them. In a solemn line the three walked across the north end of the plaza toward the highest mound in the City. As they approached the Holy Hill, which loomed blacker than night, the first Priest fell back to walk beside the old woman. He was newly a man, but already had a proud bearing. Dressed in the Priestly garments of breechcloth and belt, he also wore a small mantle of cloth decorated with beads and feathers. A carved wooden headpiece bore the image of a snake hovering beneath the rising Sun.

He spoke. "I hear you are an herbalist."

"Yes," the old woman answered sparingly. She knew the man wanted something from her.

"You have patients throughout the City, I suppose."

"Many have come under my care."

"What ails the man on the hill?"

75

Cricket Sings was relieved to know that the young man was not as intelligent as she had feared, or perhaps not experienced at intrigue. "The patient is the one who should tell you that, I think," she said firmly, but with respect.

The Priest grimaced in disappointment, then quickened his pace and reached the base of the Holy Hill just before Cricket Sings. She looked up at the steep stairs and groaned at the work her old knees would have to do. The young Priest heard and realized she would need help to climb the hill.

"You there," he called to two loitering youths. "Carry this old woman to the top, she has business with the Sun!"

The boys stepped to either side of Cricket Sings and made a cradle with their hands. Placing their crossed arms beneath the old woman's legs, they lifted her and began to climb the hill. Cricket Sings closed her eyes and made her body relax, assuming a limp posture cradled in the boys' arms. She pulled herself into her belly where her strength was hidden. She did not open her eyes or her mind until the young men placed her on her feet near the top of the Holy Hill. The two Priests had also climbed the slope and one waved the boys back down from the top. Sun had passed into Night and only a dim light lingered on the horizon. Small fires blossomed across the City as far as the old woman could see. Smoke hazed the air.

Cricket Sings heard drumming and the music of flutes as she climbed the last few steps to the top. Outlined against a fire were the leaping forms of dancers. She held her fear inside, nodded to the Priests, and walked toward the fire. A dancer turned as they approached. His face was smeared with red and black paint in stripes. The old woman met his eyes and saw the crazed look which came with visions from the holy seeds. As he shrieked and turned back to the dance, she saw beyond him a large animal roasting over the fire. With a shudder she realized that it was not an animal, but the well-formed body of a man, ribs arching over the fire. One leg had already been cut away and a Priest was hacking off pieces of meat with his hand knife. She turned her face back toward Night and felt her stomach knot with fear. Her worst suspicions about the Priesthood were true. Showing no other sign of the cold horror which had settled in her heart, the old woman made her face like stone. In her mind the mourning song was wailing.

The trio circled the crowd of celebrating men, walking to the far side of the hill. In the dim light Cricket Sings could see a rude shelter of saplings and skins. Eagle sat stolidly at the entrance, keeping guard over his father. As Moon emerged from the hut she bent double with the burden of her grief.

"How is the Sun King?" the old woman asked, startling both Eagle and Moon.

"The same, he is the same, he will be the same until he dies," moaned Moon, rocking from one foot to the other.

"Why did you bring him to this place? He would have been more comfortable in his own house."

"All his life my husband has spent the night before the Ceremony on this hill. I thought it would be fitting that he spend this night of his last festival in the place of his ancestors."

"A wise decision," murmured the herb woman as she entered the hut. She bent over the man, noting that foul herbs were no longer being burned near him. His face seemed to have fallen in around the bones. The forehead was moist, but his lips were cracked and dry. He looked like any old man of the People. She stroked his cheek for a moment, noting the creases which ran like great valleys across his face. As she stood, the old woman's head bumped against the ceiling, shaking the rude shelter. Outside, Moon and Eagle were impatient.

"My husband will die before morning?" asked Moon.

"Perhaps," was the slow answer. "I cannot say, it is a matter of waiting for the body to finish. Already his spirit is on some far road."

"No, no, no," Moon cried softly, her voice low so that the Priests waiting nearby could not hear. "This has never happened in the memory of the People. The Sun King has always died swiftly and never before at a time when there were Ceremonies to be performed. We have lived in the shelter of the Sun's good will. Now there will be no Ceremony, Sun will be displeased and bad times will fall upon the People. The wind has whispered to me these past few nights." She slumped to the ground. Turning her beautiful face up to Cricket Sings she spoke one more word. "Please. . ."

The old woman was torn. The Sun religion was the foundation upon which her life was built. The only clear path was to let the Sun King linger. Surely he would die within the next few days.

With the attention of the Priests given over to their feasting, the body could be removed to a place where the curious could be kept away. She felt the plan forming.

"Listen, Moon and Eagle. Let us enter the hut and sit quietly as though waiting for the Sun to wake. I have a plan."

She led the way with Moon and Eagle following silently behind. When they were seated in a semicircle around the empty shell of the Sun King, the herb woman spoke once more.

"Our only path, if this man does not die during the night, is to lie to both the Priests and the People. We will tell them the Sun King is dead and hide him, substituting the body of an old man who died recently." She stopped as a picture of Remember the Fish went through her thoughts. The old man had always been her friend and would want to help her now. "Eagle can then take on the role of Sun King, perform the Ceremony, and the People may never guess the true state of affairs. The omens have been very bad, I must tell you. The People are worried and need the presence of a strong King."

Eagle sat quietly. He did not look at Moon or Cricket Sings, but turned his gaze instead to the face of his father. After a long silence the youth spoke. "It is the only way. If we kill my father someone surely will know. Evil surrounds us all, but if we perform the Ceremony correctly perhaps the People will not suffer. I think the Sun might forgive me for worshipping in place of the King before the People would forgive me for killing him."

"Then it will be done," agreed Moon. "The problem is where to hide the body of the Sun King."

"We must first remove him from the care of these Priests," the herb woman instructed. "Perhaps he could be taken to his own house where he would be more comfortable? The cold and damp of this night may be too much for his weakened body."

"A good suggestion," said Eagle. His voice had taken on a commanding note. "My uncle, Bear in the Sky, must not know how serious the Sun King's illness has become until we announce the death. He has been asking questions."

"That man is one to watch," Moon agreed. "He would like to be Sun King. If he could, Bear in the Sky would murder Eagle, but the Priests know my son is vigorous and Bear in the Sky has not won their trust."

The old woman spoke. "You must be on guard despite the loyalty of the Priests. Who are the two young men who accompanied me?"

"They are childhood playmates, selected as my companions when we were very small."

"They are loyal?"

"It goes beyond loyalty. Our lives are twined together. If I die without good cause, they will search until they find the reason, be it man or spirit. There are many others who follow me in this way."

Cricket Sings looked hard at Eagle. "Do you have the good will of the People?" she posed the crucial question.

"It is widely known that Bear in the Sky is evil. He would not rule the People honestly nor lead them closer to the Sun."

Moon reached out and gently touched her dying husband's face with her hand. Her lips moved, but no sound was heard. Cricket Sings continued the plans.

"In the charnel house of my class is the body of Remember the Fish, who died two days ago. He does not resemble the Sun King, except that he is the same size. Send your two companions to me. We will fetch this body and place it in the house of the Sun King on his pallet. The two men will return to this hill and say that the Sun King must be returned to his own house where he will be protected from dampness. They will take him to the house, in case anyone is watching, but will carry him out the second door and to my house by a roundabout way. The Priests are busy with feasting. If the Sun King dies tonight it will be several days before they hold his funeral. Have your two young Priests change into clothes of the Honored class before they begin their journeys."

Moon and Eagle nodded silently.

"I will return to my family," the old woman said. "I have promised to tell a story at the fireside. Send your men to me after the dogs are asleep."

"We will do this difficult thing together, old woman, and your family will live in my protection," the young Eagle said gratefully.

"By the will of the Sun," replied the herb woman as she rose from her squatting position. Eagle and Moon stood also. At the entrance of the hut they bowed and Cricket Sings silently returned the honor before slipping into the night. She skirted the gruesome feast and reached the stairs leading downward at the southern edge of the Holy Hill. The two young Priests were waiting.

"Go," she said. "The Eagle needs you." She pointed back to the hut.

Without a word the two Priests turned and walked swiftly toward the hut. Cricket Sings made her way down the stairs, one at a time. Her legs ached and trembled, but she did not stop to rest. Her friends and family were waiting for the story. She must hide these unusual happenings as long as possible. As she descended, the old woman sang her medicine song and began to gather the story in her mind. The death of the Sun King would bring change to the People. She would tell the story of the first great Sun King who made the People One and built the City.

The plaza was dark and only a few small fires burned, surrounded by People from faraway villages. For many there would be stories and remembrances tonight. Others would drink the weak beer fermented from last year's corn and sleep drunkenly until aroused by friends to greet the Sun. Cricket Sings plodded toward the twin mounds just inside the palisade gate. The smell of death reached out to surround her. She inhaled deeply, willing her fear to pass. Once outside the palisade, she quickened her pace.

Finally her own house was visible, so safe and ordinary that the events of the past two days seemed a dream. Yet her peaceful life was now the dream and fear was real. She began to hurry faster. The fire was burning high and many had gathered for the story. She slowed her pace to a more dignified walk. Wolf Hunter was the first to hear her approaching footsteps. He turned and smiled, then bent to touch his wife on the shoulder. Excitement rippled through the seated group.

"Good evening, my loved ones," said Cricket Sings in a powerful voice. "I have come to tell you the story of the first great Sun King of the People, the man who came from the south." She walked to the door of the house and set her bag inside, then straightened her overdress. The water jug stood just outside the door and she picked up a small bowl and dipped a drink, then refilled the bowl and carried it with her to an empty pallet at the fireside. Closing her eyes, the old woman began to hum her song, lost in the rhythm. She did not hear the others singing until she stopped. The People continued humming softly.

"When Sun and Moon first made the People, they gave a Sun in the World to find the correct ways of life. This Sun King lived in the south, where he was close to light and warmth. He built high hills to be even closer to the Creator. As the People spread over the World, the old ones sometimes died before they could tell their stories and thus some People did not know how to worship. They wandered with no sense of their place in the World. Because these People had no Priests to determine the seasons, they could not plant or harvest corn. Their gardens were poor. When People do not have food they are weak and sickly.

"In the south the Sun King heard of this grave state of affairs. He could not allow his People to forget their heritage. It happened that this great King had a younger brother, a man of forceful demeanor, much concerned with laws and rightness. The Sun King, considering the need of the People in the North for one to remember their Ceremonies, found the solution and appointed his brother as Sun King in the north.

"A small army was gathered, but this army did not carry axes or spears. Instead, the men were loaded with seed corn. Artisans were chosen from those who volunteered for adventure and the army set forth in boats to sail across a salty lake to the end of our great river called Father of Waters. At each camping place on the journey upriver the Sun King taught the People their heritage.

"They looked for a place to build a city for there were only small villages in this uncivilized country. From the People who lived on the river the Sun King learned that to the north there was a fine site where two great rivers joined to make the Father of Waters. It was said that the wide plains of this region would make good corn fields. The Sun King found a man to guide him to this place and they traveled north into the beginning of winter. The People of the Sun were farmers, not hunters, and they had no fall crops to replenish their dwindling food supplies. They pleaded with their leader to eat the precious seed corn, but he refused and reminded them that corn is sacred to the Sun. When they came to the broad plain for which they had searched, the black soil was covered with snow. A tribe of hunters lived at this place and they taught the People of the south to hunt. Although many grew thin and pale, no one died of hunger that winter.

"When spring came and the weather was good for travel, the new Sun King sent word by messenger to all the People. They came from great distances. In a yellow feather cape the Sun King came forth from his rude hut. He divined that the time was right for planting and decreed which areas would form the corn fields. When the planting was finished the Sun King began to think about the City. After considering all possible places, he found a powerful site for the Holy Hill. The People made war on those who did not follow the Sun and took slaves. The children of those slaves are the Ordinaries, who even now labor in the service of the Sun because it is their only hope of holiness.

"When the Hill was well begun, the King turned his attention to the need of the City for trade. He sent emissaries, and traders began to gather here. The Sun King chose his sister for a bride and she was our first Moon. Dark and beautiful, she bore him many children, so the future was assured. This Moon remembered the stories of her grandmother and each night she told the history of the People." The old woman stopped for a moment, looking around at the faces of the young women who would be grandmothers in years hence.

"After many years the Sun King grew old. The Holy Hill had become very high and although the Priests cut steps into the side the Sun King was too weak to worship. He was carried everywhere by his sons. The eldest son was named Eagle and he was the man who built our first Sun Circle to foretell the seasons. To celebrate this feat, the father declared that the day the Sun shone farthest would each year be a great festival.

"The Sun King knew his time in the World was nearly over. A wise and thoughtful man, he instructed young Eagle in the ways of the People. A group of four Warriors conspired to kill the old man because they felt he was no longer powerful. They poisoned him by putting something evil into his corn. The body was placed in the charnel house and everyone thought the Sun King had died naturally. The new King immediately began to construct a holy place for his father. Because the dead man had come from the south, a large pole was placed exactly at the center of the southern edge of the City. A hill was then built on this site.

"The first Sun King had been a man who appreciated beautiful women, as what good man does not? Many young women came forward to accompany the dead man into Night. They were given the seeds which make holy visions. At the height of their excitement, they were taken to the Holy Hill and killed at Sunrise. The youngest maiden was a Seer and in her last moments she revealed her visions of the ugly deed of the traitors. The body of the old man was placed on a bed of the finest shell beads for burial. He was accompanied by his favorite servant. Nearby, the handmaidens were laid together. The four criminals were behanded and beheaded in the plaza in full view of the People. Their bodies were buried in the new hill, but their heads and hands were tied on stakes erected in the plaza and rotted there in the Sun as a reminder to those who would engage in treachery.

"So the new Sun King began his rule and he was powerful, but no one could equal the feats of our first great Sun King, who united the People and built our City. As we rejoice in this day when the Sun shines farthest we should also remember to honor the first Sun King. He is with us in the light of his Creator.

"Now you must go to your own fires on this chilly night. In the morning we will walk at the first hint of light to the great circle where the People gather as One to greet the Sun."

Cricket Sings returned from her story as though she had been in another land. She blinked twice, then looked around at her friends and family. As on other nights, the young women rose first, followed by their husbands and parents. Cricket Sings noticed that Touch the Hawk left with the family of Running Water. He walked very close to Talking Tree. When only Wolf Hunter and Doe Eyes were left, the family remained silent, enjoying the fire, the cool night, and the stars. Finally Daughter stirred in her sleep and Doe Eyes rose to carry the child into the house.

"Mother, I would like to sleep," she said. "Will you be awake on this smallest of nights?"

"Yes, child, I will keep watch for the morning. Sleep well."

As Wolf Hunter rose to follow his wife, Cricket Sings detained him with a hand on his arm.

"Wait, my son. We have matters to discuss."

It was not often that the old woman called upon Wolf Hunter. Now there was a note of urgency in her voice. She felt his arm tense.

"I have secrets which are not your burden, but I need your help tonight. I have no other son." Cricket Sings let go of his arm.

The young man nodded. "I will help, old woman. Your family has become my own."

"Good." She paused, then began again. "I have an errand for you. The Little One who is the child of Carries Baskets will be my apprentice."

"Doe Eyes told me. Why not wait until after the Ceremony to take an apprentice?"

"No!" Her voice was sharp. "I must have help now!" Then her face and voice softened. "Perhaps you could take a bag of corn to their house after the Ceremony tomorrow and bring the child to me?"

"That is not a problem, I will be glad to help."

"There is something else." She hesitated, gathering courage. "Two youths will come to this house when the dogs are asleep. In the charnel house of our family is the body of a man who died two days ago. You will take them there. They will steal this body and later will return with a living man who will hide in our house. Your wife and children may be endangered if this exchange does not go smoothly. No one, not even those of our family, can know what we do tonight. Do you understand?"

Wolf Hunter's broad face, which usually held an expression of friendly interest, was now drawn tight with fear, shadowed by firelight.

"I will help you, Mother, but promise me that if I do these things my son and daughter will live."

She put her gnarled hand on his arm again. "I cannot promise, Wolf Hunter. I can only say that if our secrets are kept the danger will be less. You are the only man I trust to help."

"My son is the last of his family, but I will follow you in this matter because I have seen your wisdom in the past."

Cricket Sings sighed with relief. "Thank you, son. These burdens have been very heavy for an old woman with no strong husband to help."

The two sat waiting by the fire. Once when a leaf crackled near the road the old woman reached out to Wolf Hunter and gripped his arm, but it was only a dog turning round and round to find a comfortable bed. The night closed about the People as they withdrew to their houses to sleep fitfully. When the stars had spun half their course, the two young men silently appeared. The old woman motioned them closer, then indicated with signs that they were to follow Wolf Hunter.

"Go swiftly and silently," she instructed in a whisper.

The three men disappeared. She waited a long time while the stars whirled. When Wolf Hunter returned the odor of death was on him.

"Go to the lake," she whispered. "You smell of the charnel house. Wash in the water, your clothes as well as your body. We will hang them inside the house and no one will know."

Wolf Hunter nodded and once again disappeared. The old woman entered the house and began to arrange the pallets and fur robes on her side of the house. Doe Eyes and the children were sleeping soundly. Cricket Sings created a corner which would cradle the dying Sun King during his brief time left in the World. As she finished, the two young Priests returned, carrying their burden. She ushered them into the house and they laid the Sun King in the corner she had prepared. As they left the house she followed, whispering of the need to wash off the smell of death. They nodded and bowed before walking toward the lake.

She returned to the Sun King, who was breathing with difficulty, and covered him almost completely with fur robes, folding them to allow only a small hole for air. Then she stood in the door, noting with satisfaction that the outline of the man could not be seen. The heavy robes muffled his loud breathing. The old woman was sitting by the fire when Wolf Hunter returned, and she motioned him to her side.

"The man is hidden in our house," she said, putting her hand against Wolf Hunter's mouth so he could not interrupt. "He is important, but he is dying. No one must know that he is here." She released her hand.

"I would like to sleep with my wife. Will you watch alone?"

"Yes, I like the Night."

As he rose, Wolf Hunter began to sing his medicine chant in a small voice. If death came unexpectedly, the song would already be flying to guide his soul into the long night. As a counterpart, Cricket Sings chanted her comfort song until she heard Wolf Hunter snoring regularly.

CHAPTER NINE
Celebration

Cricket Sings woke with a start. She was very cold and the fire was only a red glow in the ashes. She had been asleep, sitting up straight in the Night. Her knees were drawn up under her chin, which rested comfortably on top of them. In the east the sky was glowing.

"Wake up, Wolf Hunter, wake up," she whispered loudly. "The morning approaches."

The old woman stood carefully, placing her hands on her hips and stretching her stiff back like a bow. Wolf Hunter was awake and she heard the noises caused by sleepers rising.

"I am here," he said, letting the old woman know he was ready for any event.

She scanned the surroundings, but the streets were quiet. Here and there fires burned, sending tendrils of smoke up into the calm air. Then they heard the first thump of the drum, like a great heart beating for the People.

"We must hurry to greet the Sun," sang the old woman as she walked to the door of her house and peered inside.

Doe Eyes had heard the summons of the drum and was dressing her unprotesting children in their best garments. When the children were ready, Doe Eyes walked out of the house, leaving Son and Daughter to drowse for a few moments more. Silently the old woman and her daughter walked to the toilet area. They returned to the house without speaking, and Doe Eyes avoided looking at the bundle of skins in the corner as she picked up Son and carried him outside. Sleepy Daughter hung whining from her mother's hand. They were ready.

Wolf Hunter had also been to the toilet. Upon his return, he went into the house and reappeared in his cape to assume his place among the People. Cricket Sings picked up her bag from inside the door, stopping for a moment to listen for the breathing of the Sun King. She heard a wheeze, then for a long moment nothing, until she thought perhaps he might never breathe again. But he did, and she nodded as she left the house, flipping the new doorscreen neatly into place. She led her family into the growing crowd of People streaming toward the palisade gate. Across the City the People rose and joined to welcome the Sun, called by the deep-voiced drums.

They assembled in a great meadow to the west of the Holy Hill. No one spoke, not even a dog barked to mar the sacred moments. The field was full and still the People came, until the crowd reached from the great circle of poles, which the Priests used to determine the seasons, all the way back to the main plaza. The sky was very light now and a rustle of feathers could be heard. The song of a redwing blackbird rippled, then stopped. Tension gripped the crowd, the silence heightened by the anticipation of ecstasy. To the east a path opened and Priests approached the great pillars, those of lesser rank coming first, followed by men of higher station. All wore feathered capes of great beauty. The newly initiated Priests had short capes of brown feathers and stood in a circle just inside the observatory. At the sight of the Sun King, glowing in his yellow feather mask and full-length golden cape, a roar of pleasure grew from the People, echoing from the river to the hills.

"Ahhh . . .Ahhh . . ." sighed Cricket Sings, too much a woman of the People to do anything but adore this glorious figure, their Sun in the World.

Everywhere the People rejoiced. Cricket Sings saw the Priests place the Sun King in his special chair. They began pulling the fibrous rope which tugged him into the sky. His cape fluttered in the first stirring of morning air as he hung and swayed from the tallest pole. To the east four small clouds stretched like pink fingers, an auspicious omen, for rather than letting himself be swept above the horizon by natural forces the Son was reaching to pull himself upward. The Sun King held out his arms to the east, slowly raising them as he pulled the golden tip of the Sun away from Night.

The People shrieked and screamed, all at once and together. Old and young, pregnant mothers and proud Warriors danced and cried, thanking Sun for his presence. After a time the Celebration grew calmer and less frenzied. Cricket Sings noticed that the Sun King and Priests had slipped away. The crowd began to move back through the central City toward their homes and she grabbed Daughter's shoulder so the child would not be swept away and lost.

"This has been a most wonderful Celebration," she shouted to Doe Eyes and Wolf Hunter. Her whole body felt strong and warm.

"Yes," answered the young woman. "I think we have some matters to take care of at home." Her voice was flat and she looked boldly into her mother's eyes.

Wolf Hunter suddenly grabbed his wife by the arm and squeezed so hard that she gasped in pain.

"We will say no more, woman," he muttered angrily under his breath and Doe Eyes nodded, tucking her chin down onto her chest.

The crowd had thinned by the time the family reached the plaza. Gamblers were already playing their games. A win on the day of the Sun Celebration was an omen of good fortune in the coming year. A shout went up from the crowd surrounding the chunky field. Wolf Hunter watched the players as he walked past, but his father had been a gambler like so many men of the People and the young man had known hungry winters after the loss of the family hunting tools. He did not stop.

"Look, there is One Eye!" exclaimed Cricket Sings. She walked faster, weaving between the People.

One Eye was sitting in her familiar place in front of the stall where her daughters sold age-old medicines. She looked smaller and older than ever and was dressed in a fine cape of tanned deerskin which flared on the ground around her. Her white hair was braided and adorned with feathers.

"Who approaches?" she asked as she heard the steps coming closer. "Ah, it is you, my friend Cricket Sings. Do you have time to sit with an old woman?"

"I do. There is news that may not please you, but at least it will be interesting." Cricket Sings folded her legs and sat beside her friend, laying her medicine bag to one side. On second thought, she reached for the bag and rummaged around inside, removing the three objects which One Eye had given her the day before. Wolf Hunter and Doe Eyes, carrying the children, walked up to the old women.

"Mother, we are going back to our house to prepare for the feast," Doe Eyes said meekly, her face downcast.

"A good idea, daughter. There is corn meal for breads and I will make yellow flower tea. I will not be long here, please do not leave for the feast without me."

"We will wait for you, old woman," answered Wolf Hunter. "Come wife, we have work to do."

The young couple walked toward the palisade gate. They were in no hurry and lingered to enjoy the sights and sounds of the festival. Cricket Sings waited until they were out of hearing range before rustling her overdress to let One Eye know that something was about to happen.

"I have tried your teas, my friend," she said in her loudest old woman voice. "Your tastes are not to my liking, so I will return these herbs and instead give you some yellow flowers so you may drink my favorite yellow flower tea during the winter."

She grasped One Eye's withered-looking left hand and placed the three objects in the other woman's curved palm. One Eye reached for her medicine bag and hid the bark and the small tied package which concealed the tiny black pottery bottle. Carefully, One Eye tightened the neck of her bag and both women replaced their pouches at their sides.

"It is too bad you don't like my tea," One Eye said. "I would like to try this yellow flower tea of which you are so fond."

"Well, here is what I have in my bag," Cricket Sings replied, removing a loosely woven pouch of plant fibers which contained the dried flowers. "I can give you more tonight if you like. My sister Running Water, you may remember her, is having a feast today. I tasted the venison and it is some of the best I have ever eaten."

"You are wise, always thinking of your stomach," laughed One Eye. "We will talk later, then?"

"Yes, later." She grabbed her bag and unfolded her legs from the mat, wiggling as she stood to shake her old bones back into their accustomed position. Touching the top of One Eye's white head she said, "My friend, I will see you this evening at the fire."

"Yes, my children and I enjoy your stories."

Cricket Sings walked slowly away. She noticed the rich clothing and myriad painted designs with which some revelers had decorated themselves. She would paint her own face, and perhaps her grandchildren, too. As she passed through the palisade gate the odor of roasting meat was strong, but she could not tell whether it was from her sister's fire or that of a neighbor. She saw Running Water turning the meat, which had roasted to a crisp brown. It was evident that much tasting had been necessary because one end of the haunch was stripped to the bone.

"Hello, sister," called Cricket Sings as she passed. "We will return with the corn breads and yellow flowers for tea."

For once, Running Water was too busy to talk and merely waved in recognition before turning back to her work. Cricket Sings ignored the growling in her stomach and turned the corner toward her own house. Doe Eyes was baking corn breads on a flat stone by the fire. Son was propped in the shade against the house and Little Daughter played in the dirt at her mother's feet. Suddenly the herb woman felt a sense of dread. She did not know what she would find inside the house and her stomach rolled over and over. Wolf Hunter was nowhere to be seen. Perhaps he had gone to fetch Little One, she thought, but at that moment he emerged from the house. He held one hand over his head to draw attention, then nodded almost imperceptibly. She knew that the Sun King was dead and his heir would now reign. Perhaps the old man had died even before Eagle had welcomed the Sun. She felt cold as she thought of the night to come. They would have to return the dead King's body to his house and replace Remember the Fish's body in the charnel house. She felt danger closing around her and walked very fast the last few steps to her house, trying to put the persistent worries out of her thoughts. When she reached the fire she was almost running.

Doe Eyes was patting out corn breads carefully between her hands, making each one perfectly round and flat. A bowl at her side held the mixture of ground corn and water. In front of her, with its far side resting against the coals of the fire, a flat stone held a baked bread which was ready to remove. Deftly, Doe Eyes flipped the raw corn bread onto one hand, slid the baked bread from the stone, and slapped the other into its place. Then she placed the delicately browned bread on top of a stack on a dull black plate at her side. She looked up at her mother and smiled. Cricket Sings realized that Doe Eyes knew the mysterious man in the house was dead. The young woman scooped another handful of dough from the bowl and began to pat out a corn bread.

"Welcome, mother, I am almost finished here and we will be ready to go when you have gathered your herbs for tea."

Wolf Hunter hunkered down next to his wife, moving the plate of finished breads to get closer. Daughter immediately ran and climbed into his lap, cooing and cuddling joyfully. Cricket Sings sat next to Wolf Hunter.

"Our visitor has left, then?" she asked in a small, tight voice.

"Yes," answered Wolf Hunter. "However, he left something behind which our two friends must collect in the night."

"Perhaps one will come to investigate and we will tell him of this day's events," answered the old woman with a sigh of relief.

"I am ready." Doe Eyes slapped the last corn bread on top of the stack.

"Ah, child, you scared me," said the old woman with a start. "Wolf Hunter, I keep forgetting the Little One. Could you walk to the Ordinaries' huts after the feast and bring the child to me?" She gave her son-in-law her sweetest smile.

Wolf Hunter laughed out loud. "You are such a tricky old woman, who knows what you will do next? Of course I will fetch the child, but she must have a bath before she sleeps in the house. Perhaps you could meet us at the sweat house? That way I can go to the plaza and visit with my brothers."

"An excellent idea. I think the child can walk from the sweat house to our home. We will talk more after the feast."

Everyone stood up and Cricket Sings went into the house to get a large packet of yellow flower tea herbs. She glanced at the body hidden in the corner. It is better not to brood on danger, she thought. Leaving the house, the old woman picked up the plate of corn breads and her bag. Wolf Hunter carried his son because the family would be gathered and he was proud of his lusty Warrior child. Daughter, in a dress trimmed with red and yellow quill embroidery, toddled reluctantly beside her mother.

"No!" she said emphatically when Doe Eyes attempted to hold her hand. The child broke loose and ran forward to walk with her grandmother.

"Humph," snorted Doe Eyes. "The child grows more like you every day, Mother. She is stubborn and willful."

"In that, she is also like her mother!" the old woman replied.

Delicious cooking smells filled the air. The sky was as blue as Cricket Sings could remember and small white clouds flew peacefully, causing shadows here and there but carrying no rain to spoil the day. The People were gathered with their families to feast and tell stories. Tents made of skin were pitched next to many houses, indicating the presence of out-of-town relatives. At one fire a dog was roasting and two small girls sat fascinated as their brother turned the spit. Soon their father would carve the first pieces of crisp meat. A crowd had gathered in front of Running Water's house. Yellow Dog stood with his two sons and Shade of the Tree. The shell trader, Touch the Hawk, was enjoying the company of Running Water's marriageable daughters.

"Yellow Dog!" shouted Wolf Hunter. "How are you?"

He handed the cradleboard to Doe Eyes, then ran ahead. The two men met at the road, hugging and pounding each other on the back. Arm in arm they walked to the fire. The host, Starving Creek, joined the other two men. As Cricket Sings, Doe Eyes and the two children reached the fire, Running Water bustled out of the house.

"Well, hello, sister and niece. Little Daughter, over there are some other children, play gently with them and I will give you a surprise after we eat."

Running Water gently ushered Daughter toward a grassy area where the three children of a neighbor were playing with cornhusk dolls.

"Well, sister, come and sit with me. Ah, I see you have brought corn breads, that is wonderful. They look so crusty and brown. I know Doe Eyes baked them; you were never that interested in cooking. Here, sit and rest. The meal is almost ready and I have the water hot for yellow flower tea."

Obediently, Doe Eyes and Cricket Sings walked to the opposite side of the fire where the women were sitting in a row. On the end, next to pretty Talking Tree, sat Touch the Hawk. With one ear he listened to the men's conversation, throwing in a comment from time to time so that he would seem to be a part of the talk. His real attention was focused on the young woman at his side. Demurely, she kept her shining eyes averted from her suitor and sat erect, careful not to lean too close.

Cricket Sings nodded when she saw the pot of water steaming at the edge of the coals. She reached into her bag and drew out the large packet of yellow flower tea, opened it, and dropped half the contents into the water to brew. Then she sat next to her sister, whose flow of talk continued.

"Well, I saw this nice young man Touch the Hawk at your story last night and invited him to join our feast today. I thought that since he is an acquaintance of yours, sister, he would feel more comfortable with us. Such a waste it would be, not to eat all of this good meat. I think we are ready. If anyone else comes they can just take the leavings. Oh, shh." She leaned close to Cricket Sings and spoke in a very small voice. "I saved some dried pumpkin from last fall and made a delicous pudding with roots and a bird egg. See, there in that covered dish." She pointed to the dish at the very edge of the fire.

Running Water stood and signaled her husband to begin cutting the meat. Starving Creek looked as though even if he ate the entire haunch it would make only a little difference in his skinny contours.

"People," he began, and they were immediately quiet, even Running Water. "We have this morning celebrated the return of Sun and now we are with our beloved family. We celebrate the taste of venison and corn, the good hum of conversation, the life of the People. Let us rejoice as we eat this meal and thank Sun in the Sky for the richness of our lives."

With that, he drew his knife from a sheath at his hip and began to slice the meat. Running Water handed him a corn bread and he placed a thick slice of brown, juicy venison on top, then walked around the fire to hand the first slice to the guest, Touch the Hawk. The young man accepted with a silent nod. The next slices were passed around the fire to the other men, then Starving Creek cut his own large slice, handed the knife to Running Water, and returned to his seat. She cut a tiny piece and called Daughter, who came running from her play with a dirty face and a large grin. The child grabbed the meat and ran at once to her father, sitting in the curve of his lap to eat. The women were served, and while Doe Eyes ate she gave Son her breast so that he would not grow hungry and fretful. The sounds of smacking lips and sighs filled the air. Conversation came to a halt. When the eating slowed, over half the large haunch had been consumed.

Night Bird, the younger daughter of Running Water, rolled onto her back on the ground and rubbed her belly, which stuck out as though she had swallowed a pumpkin. Daughter copied her cousin, giggling when the adults laughed.

"A delicious meal, sister," praised Cricket Sings. "I have never tasted better."

A murmur of agreement passed around the fire and Running Water's chubby face beamed.

"Thank you, thank you, kind People. I will fetch some bowls and we will have a little of Cricket Sings' yellow flower tea, which I like more than any tea I have tasted. So we will have two best things today and this will truly be a Celebration."

She rushed into the house to get her tea bowls, several of which looked very new and had apparently been purchased for this occasion. Night Bird rose to help her mother and returned with four bowls which she filled by dipping into the simmering tea. The first bowls were handed to the men, starting once again with Touch the Hawk. Running Water hurried out of the house carrying six more bowls, five of which she filled for the women. The last was handed to young Wounded Deer, who had been sitting quietly next to his father Yellow Dog during the meal. The child was recovering from his illness, but still appeared pale and weak. Cricket Sings thought that soon she would advise Yellow Dog to take his son home to rest.

The shadows began to grow as Sun reached toward the west. Members of the family decided that perhaps the time had come for a nap. Yellow Dog was first to yawn and others followed his example.

"Yellow Dog, your child looks tired to me," said Cricket Sings, offering her suggestion. "I am in need of a nap. Perhaps we will walk home together?"

"Of course," Yellow Dog replied immediately. He reached out to touch Wounded Deer's forehead with his large hand. "Let us walk to our camp, son."

The boy immediately stood and waited for his mother and brother to stretch and join them. Cricket Sings grabbed her sister's hand and squeezed in thanks.

"Running Water has prepared the finest feast I ever tasted," she repeated and the family answered once more with affirmative nods and grunts.

"My belly is tight as a drum," announced Wolf Hunter as he stood and offered his hand to help his wife up. Doe Eyes grasped it and pulled herself to a standing position, Son's cradleboard in the curve of the other arm. Wolf Hunter took the cradleboard as Doe Eyes straightened her wrinkled overdress.

Cricket Sings sighed. She knew she would have to rise, and forewarning prickles in her legs gave notice that such movement would be painful. With a grunt she rolled onto her hands and knees, letting her belly hang down in mock fullness, then with a comic heave she tried to rise to her feet.

"Ohhh," she groaned. "I ate too much food and I cannot stand. Sister, I will just have to stay the night and eat even more. Perhaps some of that fine pumpkin pudding would help me to walk better in the morning."

Her family laughed and Running Water pushed at her Sister's behind with one foot, sending her upright at once.

"Well," said Cricket Sings in mock indignation, "Sister, you do not have to push me to get me to leave. Just ask and I will go."

Running Water cut several slabs of meat from the remainder of the haunch and piled meat onto the plate which had held Doe Eyes' corn breads. She gave a like amount to Yellow Dog. Turning from the food, the plump woman hurried into her house and returned with a beautiful new corn husk doll. She called Daughter to her and the little girl immediately clasped her new baby in her arms and ran to show Doe Eyes.

With waves and reminders of the story time at dusk the families started for home. Cricket Sings glanced back. Touch the Hawk was sitting next to Talking Tree. He noticed her look and raised his hand in a wave. The old woman grinned before turning to catch up with Yellow Dog.

"Cousin," she called. "Wait for me. I am an old woman and my legs are short."

She hurried and Yellow Dog stopped to wait, letting his family walk ahead.

"You are pretty spry yet, old woman," he said in admiration as she caught up with him.

"When I want to hurry," she replied in a saucy voice, "I know how."

CHAPTER TEN
The
Second Dream

Cricket Sings was silent for a few moments before she spoke. "I have some worrying to do," she said to Yellow Dog.

"Speak, woman. It is not far to your house and I would like to walk with my son. If he becomes tired I will be able to carry him."

"I have heard a rumor of the Sun King's death. It is said that Eagle assumed the yellow cape and soon there will be a funeral."

Yellow Dog stopped in the middle of the road. The old woman watched surprise run across his face. He did not answer for a moment, and when he did speak his words were slow and careful.

"We will know tomorrow. It may be that the Priests have not made a public announcement because they want the People to enjoy their Celebration. The time for mourning will come soon enough." He walked even slower and put his hands behind his back, turning his face down to the road. He was deep in thought.

Cricket Sings nodded, then turned her own face down to the ground for several steps before speaking. "Do you remember when the last Sun King died? I was a young mother and you were but a boy."

"I do not remember the death itself, but rather the burying."

"The young women of the People, some of them mothers and wives, were taken from their families to accompany the Sun King on his long journey through Night. Only the most perfect and beautiful were chosen. I was passed over."

"You have always been a crafty woman and I do not doubt that you disguised your charms on that occasion," said Yellow Dog seriously. "You were a regal woman then and you are handsome yet."

"I smeared myself with mud and dog dung when the Priests came around to choose the proper women, but my short leg might also have made them look elsewhere. I am worried because Doe Eyes is very beautiful. She is obedient and dutiful, but she may also be a woman who would consider dying for the Sun King an honor. She is the last of my children, Yellow Dog." The old woman's voice broke with anguish. In a moment she was calmer and continued. "Without her tender care Son and Daughter will surely die."

Yellow Dog was silent. His own young wife was also pleasing to the eye. The answer, when it came, was slow and hesitant.

"I think we should not worry until the Priests announce that the Sun King is dead. At that time they will begin arrangements for the funeral."

Cricket Sings nodded miserably. "But if they choose my daughter we may not have time to take her away from the City."

"Wolf Hunter may want to join me in trading, and his family could travel as mine does; but then you would have no one to care for you in your old age."

"If Doe Eyes goes with the Sun King . . ." she hesitated. "I am taking an apprentice, the daughter of an Ordinary. She is young, but dutiful like my own daughter. I could also decide to die if I become unable to care for myself."

"It is settled, then. We will speak with Wolf Hunter about this matter. I could use his help and he will find more excitement traveling than hoeing corn."

They had reached Cricket Sings' house. Wolf Hunter was inside, helping his wife settle the children for a nap. He came out with Son's soiled diaper clenched in his outstretched hand.

"Phew!" he said loudly. "A child who can do this is very powerful!"

Setting the diaper carefully on the ground at the corner of the house, he walked to the road to join the two conspirators. As he approached, Cricket Sings spoke in low tones.

"Wolf Hunter, we were wondering what will happen at the funeral of the Sun King. Your young wife is very beautiful."

"Yes, that is true."

"You have never had a King die in your lifetime, but in my youth the Sun King died and many young women of the People were killed to accompany him. Not just maidens were taken, but also young mothers if they were beautiful of face and body." Her voice was tight with fear.

"They will not have Doe Eyes." Wolf Hunter's body was stiff and proud.

Yellow Dog grabbed his shoulder roughly. "This scheming old woman has a plan. You will join me on a trading expedition. You are a strong man and we will find much adventure. My family travels with me, and with their help we will be able to care for Son and Daughter."

Wolf Hunter shifted his weight from foot to foot. His answer was unsure. "I will think tonight and talk with Doe Eyes."

"We may have to move quickly if the Priests do not give notice of their intent," urged Cricket Sings.

"We will all keep our ears open," Yellow Dog added, turning toward Wolf Hunter. "After the story tonight I will walk to the plaza. It may be that I will want to eat some Holy Seeds and talk with my ancestors." Wolf Hunter's son was lagging behind the Basket Maker family. "My son is still weak from his illness and I must carry him. We will return at dusk." With a wave, Yellow Dog trotted onto the road and swung his son into his arms.

Wolf Hunter turned to Cricket Sings. His face was tired and there were dark circles beneath his eyes. "I had not thought this death would bring misfortune to the People. The Sun King and Priests have always protected us from evil."

"If you wish to have grandchildren do not bend to the Priests' will. I do not want my daughter sacrificed."

"Mother of my Beloved, you are a wise woman, but willful and proud. I think our plan is sufficient for now. We must collect our tool kits and hide grain in small packages. I will speak with my brothers about a boat. It may be that the swiftest escape is a trading trip upriver."

"You are a Warrior and I will trust your judgment in such things. I have grown to love you like my own son because of the good care you give your wife and children." There were tears in the old woman's voice.

Wolf Hunter reached out with his right hand and found Cricket Sings' boney fingers waiting in midair.

"We will not die, grandmother," he said, grasping her hand firmly. "We have known hard times before."

"Never this hard," the old woman whispered. Tears gathered at the corners of her eyes. "Now," she said suddenly, straightening and wiping a teardrop from the end of her nose with a forefinger. "We must continue our lives as though nothing has changed, except that we will be ready to leave on an extended journey at short notice."

Wolf Hunter squatted by the fire. Cricket Sings walked to the woodpile and picked up an armful of branches. She laid two pieces of wood on top of the coals, close together so they would catch and burn, then piled the others next to her pallet where they would be handy. In a loud voice she said, "Well, shall we fetch my new apprentice and wash her so that she will not bring fleas into our house?"

"An excellent idea. Meet me at the sweathouse when enough time has passed for me to walk to the Ordinary's and back."

"I will be there, son."

Wolf Hunter walked toward the road and turned south. The sun was warm and Cricket Sings felt drowsy. Her eyes were shutting and her head jerked once, then again. She decided to give in to the delicious sleepiness. Pushing and pulling the pallets until they were stretched end to end in the warm Sunlight, she took off her overdress, rolled it, and tucked the resulting bundle under her head for comfort. She closed her eyes.

Cricket Sings' soul began to wander. She flew up from her old, frail body. The spirit body was new and both legs were strong and straight. She saw the World through a misty night as she passed the palisade gate. A spirit loomed toward her out of the mist, but she had known this one before and was not afraid. She moved across the deserted plaza, angling toward the mound which held the house of the Sun King. A sick feeling passed through the spirit body as she neared the foot of the stairs, but she was strong and climbed with a powerful rhythm. Reaching the top, she turned left to the house.

The shadow of a Priest stood before the door. Cricket Sings passed through him and into the house. She heard soft weeping. Moon was crouched low in a corner, sobbing into her hands. The body, wrapped in reed mats which hid the face, lay before her. In her grief, Moon reached up and pulled a hank of hair out of her head. Other black tufts lay scattered across the the floor. Her clothing was torn and there were long scratches across her cheeks and up her arms.

The spirit woman drew back from Moon's pain, pulling herself out the door. She lifted into the air and threw herself to the top of the Holy Hill. A bonfire leapt, as grotesque figures danced in circles. The Priests were masked and dressed in costumes which concealed their true shape. Some were feasting on the smooth brown bodies of the People. They turned and came toward her, grabbing with hands that felt like winter.

Suddenly, she was awake and back in her body. Her heart was beating wildly. Dazed, she sat up. Sun had moved to the west and a tree shadowed the fireplace. The cool shade and the dream had wakened her. She raised her groggy head. The sweathouse. Why should she be there? Oh yes. She had to meet Wolf Hunter. She would be late. Sitting up, she wiggled the kinks out of her back. The spirit body had been strong and now this sagged old woman was a disappointment. Still half in the spirit world, she stood and walked to the south.

Wolf Hunter was sitting under a tree next to the sweathouse talking with the new apprentice. Cricket Sings waved when she saw them. She heard Wolf Hunter's calm voice.

"Here comes the old woman, Little One. She will be your mother now."

"I already love Cricket Sings," answered the child. "She has healed my foot. My mother says I have been given the opportunity to repay a great debt. I am honored."

"Thank you, child," said Cricket Sings softly.

"I am not afraid to have you know I am loyal," the child replied, looking up to the old woman with a solemn face.

Wolf Hunter threw back his head and loosed a bellowing laugh. "I will have to have more sons to keep ahead of such women. I am going to the plaza; tell my wife I will be home before the story." He gave Cricket Sings a serious look, ruffled the Little One's hair and strode away toward the City.

Cricket Sings helped Little One take off her deerskin rags, which were caked with dirt. The child would need a new set of clothes, she thought. Perhaps Running Water would have castoffs from her nearly grown daughters. She led the way into the sweathouse. They were alone and the steamy atmosphere soon cleansed their bodies. Little One touched the thatch, then pushed hard, trying to make the roof move. She could not. Laughing, the two hobbled from the hut.

"Let's go to the lake and rinse off this sweat," the herb woman suggested. "You can leave your old clothing here and wear my overdress home. I will speak with my sister about a new dress for you."

The child nodded obediently and went to the lake. She splashed water onto her skinny chest, careful to keep her healing foot out of the water. Cricket Sings followed and slowly rubbed the cold water over her wrinkles, remembering the days when the flesh had been smooth and tight on her bones. She thought of Sand Crane and nodded. Tonight she would tell their story. She sighed.

"Well, Little One, I think it is time to go home."

She left the water, followed by her new apprentice, and walked to the sweathouse. Pulling on her dress, she shrugged to settle it into place, then helped Little One with the overdress. It dragged on the ground. The Little One was hidden in the folds. Cricket Sings took the child's hand and they both limped toward the house.

Sun was sliding down the sky, but on this day of Celebration Night was long in coming. Cricket Sings could see Running Water, Starving Creek and their two daughters sitting at her fireplace. Fear was hard in her chest as she realized they might have discovered the dead man inside the house.

"Sister!" she called.

Running Water looked up.

"Perhaps you have some castoff clothing for this child?"

"I think there is a dress or two my daughters wore when they were young. Night Bird, go and fetch those two dresses you have outgrown and bring them here. Your aunt has taken an apprentice; she will be a new cousin for you. Go now, run!"

The girl ran toward the palisade with long leaps.

"That one will make a good dancer," said the herb woman, looking after the girl.

"Perhaps," answered her mother. "She is too young now. I would like to keep her for a few more summers. If she dances she will marry within the year."

Doe Eyes came out of the house yawning and rubbing her face sleepily.

"I had a good nap," she said. "We were very tired. Son and Daughter are still asleep."

"They will wake soon, I have no doubt," said Running Water. "They are powerful children and always hungry."

Cricket Sings folded her legs and sat near the fire. Little One stood with her hands behind her back, head hanging low. She rubbed the dirt with one bare toe.

"Ah, my child, come here," said the old woman. "We must do something with your hair. I fear it is too matted for combing, but perhaps we can cut off the worst and let it grow."

Little One nodded, head still turned down, and took two steps forward. The herb woman rose and went into her house. She felt a shudder when she saw the motionless pile of robes in the corner. Picking up her comb and knife, she returned to the fire, beckoning the child to sit in front of her. The old woman began to comb Little One's hair, hacking off large mats until she could pass the comb across the child's head easily. Now the hair was uneven and Cricket Sings clicked her tongue. She made a neat part down the center of the girl's head and looked for bugs. There were three and she squashed them between her thumb and forefinger, throwing the carcasses into the fire. The family sat in companionable silence. For once, even Running Water had no words.

"Hello, look who is here!" Wolf Hunter was accompanied by Touch the Hawk and both men wore wide grins.

Talking Tree immediately hid her pretty face in the folds of her dress and giggled. Running Water elbowed her daughter in the ribs and the young woman assumed a more dignified face and demeanor.

"Touch the Hawk," Running Water said coquettishly, "it is good to see you again this evening."

"And it is good to be a part of your family once more," he replied, taking a seat beside Starving Creek.

Wolf Hunter went to his wife and picked up one thick braid, letting it slide through his fingers until it dropped gently onto her shoulder. She looked up at him and smiled. He sat beside her.

"Here comes the one with swift feet," said Cricket Sings as Night Bird ran toward the fire. The old woman turned to Little One. "Go behind the house and see if the dresses fit, then bring my overdress back so the night will not chill me."

The child did as she was told, glancing thankfully at those who sat around the fire. Night Bird followed Little One around the corner of the house. From the south the Yellow Dog and Basket Maker families were approaching, and One Eye, accompanied by two daughters, arrived at the same time. Friends and neighbors gathered, finding seats around the fire. Cricket Sings closed her eyes and thought of the story. When all were quiet, she opened her eyes and looked around. As she spoke the first words, Little One and Night Bird crept from behind the house to the edge of the circle.

CHAPTER ELEVEN
Stories and Songs

"When each grandmother recites her stories," droned Cricket Sings, "she must also tell of her own life." She stopped for a moment and looked at the faces of the People she loved. She thought of how each of these women would one day tell her own stories. Smiling, the old woman continued. "Tonight I will share with you the life of Cricket Sings. My own grandmother, Bird Woman, came from a long line of healers. She taught me the stories of the People, and also the events of my early life, before the time of memory.

"My mother, Gentle Night Wind, was a healer but she had only a short life. As a young woman she was married to the Priest Blessing of the Sun and bore him two daughters. Blessing of the Sun was a very holy man and when the Sun King died he offered his young wife as a sacrifice to accompany the King into his long Night. My sister Running Water and I were left motherless. When our father turned increasingly to holy thoughts, Bird Woman came and took us to live in her house.

"Unlike other grandmothers, she had no daughters living with her and thus had to find her own way in the World. Instead of taking her payment for healing and medicines in fine goods, she asked for meat or corn. My first memories are of walking a very long distance to corn fields to hoe in the dust. As we grew older,

Grandmother began to teach us the lore of the herbs, but also allowed much time for play. My legs were straight then, and Running Water and I flew like the wind when we ran.

"There was a strong tree which gave shade near our house. We would climb to the top and stand in the small branches, swaying back and forth to make our own wind. We were like birds, hopping from branch to branch and twittering. One day I was not careful and, although Running Water tried to catch me, I fell from the top of the tree to the ground. My leg twisted and snapped beneath me and the bone broke through the skin.

"Bird Woman was called. She knew I would die, but she took me into the house and found bits of cloth to wrap around the bleeding wound. She straightened the leg and tied it to sticks, so that if by chance I did not die it would grow together. An evil went into my leg and it began to swell. I do not remember pain, only the horrible dreams. Running Water sat at my side, wetting my lips with water when I cried out. The High Priest came and danced over me, and in my fever I turned away from his fearful painted face. It was decided that there was no hope for me. I was abandoned to the will of the Gods.

"A young herb woman came to the City each summer to trade for plants and ideas. She had only one eye, having lost the other to a jealous suitor. Bird Woman met her in the plaza and they spoke of medicines and life. When they talked of a granddaughter who would certainly die, One Eye offered to see the child and perhaps make a new medicine. So One Eye came to this house and found me dying of the evil in my broken leg. She was horrified by the stench, but washed her knife and my leg, and cut open the places where the evil was dwelling. She made a poultice of mouldy corn and kept this on the sore places. That night I was very close to death. The two healing women sat near me through the dark and when morning came my forehead was cool. After that, One Eye came each day to make sure the holes remained open so the evil could leave. It took almost a year and in the time the leg grew crooked, as it is today. I do not count a crooked leg important when I have been given a life which the evil would have taken.

"While Running Water was playing with the other children, I hobbled after my grandmother, learning her trade. When I reached the age of marriage I braided my hair and hoped, but no youths hid behind trees to play the flute for me. Finally, Bird Woman arranged a marriage with the Warrior Smells Like a Fish and so I became a wife without love. By this time I was an herb woman in my own right. I was stubborn and not obedient to my husband's wishes. He was an old man with rotted teeth and a stink that no sweathouse could take away. Smells like a Fish wanted to sleep with me, but I pushed him away every night and soon he began to gamble, stealing home near dawn. He gambled with his own possessions at first and won, but later he began to lose and then he took the fur robes of my grandmother so that we had nothing to keep us warm. The winter was approaching and I knew he was not a good man so I put his moccasins and hunting kit outside the door one night. In the early morning he tripped over them and cried out when he realized I did not want him. Someone said he went to the hills, but I never saw him after that.

"My sister Running Water married a good Warrior man, but then her new husband was injured in a game and lay sick in her house. It seemed that our family was cursed by sickness. Running Water bore a son and I felt the emptiness of my own belly which was made to hold many children. Each afternoon I stopped at Running Water's house to play with her son. He was a strong child with fat legs and cheeks and slanted eyes like his mother.

"Once more spring came but I did not feel it in my heart. It was the time of Celebration. Our small corn patch was planted and a cousin of my grandmother gave us a rabbit for a feast. I sat in front of our house at dusk and heard the sound of one flute playing behind the same tree from which I had fallen as a child. The song was beautiful in the evening and I had never heard such music so near before. When the rabbit was finished cooking, the flute player crept quietly away. I wondered which marriageable young woman he had been caressing with his music. Grandmother and I ate the rabbit and it was delicious.

"The next evening I was putting wood on the fire when again the music rose behind the tree. I squinted into the dusk, but could not see the player. He came each night, serenading the woman of his choice. The neighborhood was buzzing with gossip, but no one knew the identity of the flute player's beloved. The season of heat came to the City, and dust flew at every step. We hoed dirt up around the roots of the corn to keep it moist, but the leaves began to wilt. Still the unseen flute player came each evening.

"One day Grandmother came home with a strange but happy look on her face, such as I had not seen for many years. A young stone worker, Sand Crane, had approached her to ask if I would be his bride. He was the flute player behind the tree, too shy to court me in the open. So it was that we were brought together by our loneliness, and when we looked upon each other at the feast celebrating our marriage we felt a warmth which spread through our life.

"We lived together for seven summers, but in the last summer an evil grew in Sand Crane's chest and he began to cough. My grandmother and I made our best medicines while my three small children sat next to the pallet of their father. The fever stretched his body thin and made his eyes like brilliant stones set in dark circles. I prayed to the Gods but he died. One by one my children were taken with this same evil. The two sons died and only the small girl child lived. Her eyes were very big in her pinched face and it was at this time that I began to call her Doe Eyes.

"The evil spread through the City; the People died in the streets and there were no relatives to carry the bodies to the charnel houses where they might decay properly before burial. Near the very end of the evil, when only the strongest were left, my old grandmother fell ill and within a day her body was cold and stiff. It was the hardest time the People have every known. There seemed to be no end to death. Because so many were weak or dead the corn was not cared for properly and the yield was small. Even the strong starved that winter, but we were glad for the hunger. It fit the gnawing in our souls for the lost ones whose spirits wandered the City waiting for burial.

"By spring all the bodies were rotting in the charnel houses and even though the stench of death hung in the air the corn was planted. The Sun King performed the Ceremony, and life began to resume the circular shape which brings yesterday and tomorrow together. I did not take another man, but lived alone with my small daughter. We could no longer make the trips which had kept me supplied with herbs for medicines. We could only walk half a day from the City, gathering as many plants as we could on the way home. Some necessary herbs could not be found and so One Eye began to bring them to me at each Sun Ceremony.

"I thought the grief for my husband would never end, but there was much work to be done and as one grows older the time passes more swiftly. In a few summers the flute once again echoed from behind trees and this time it was Wolf Hunter playing for my daughter Doe Eyes. So now I am a grandmother and these stories fall from my lips like stones into a pond. Perhaps they will make a ripple. If you remember, tell your own grandchildren. The fire is low and I am cold. Let us get some wood and sing the old songs."

Wolf Hunter saw Cricket Sings' eyes clear and focus. He stood, walked to the woodpile, and gathered several logs into the crook of his arm. Setting two on the fire, he placed the others nearby and resumed his seat next to Doe Eyes, rubbing the soft hair on his son's head as the baby slept between them.

One Eye spoke suddenly in a voice like a dried-up leaf. "I would like to sing a song my grandmother taught me." She struggled to rise and her two daughters helped her to a standing position. The old blind woman drew a deep breath.

> Proud Sun standing in the Night
> calls his children
> People gather in the street
> coming together
> they stand arm in arm
> the People are crowded
> one duck flies low across the red east
> Sun in the World
> calls his ancestor and ours
> gently raising the God from sleep
> the People sing their joy
> new as the year
> older than memory.

The thready old voice drew the song down to a close. A murmur rippled through the group. As the old woman sank to her knees, Yellow Dog stood, his smooth body glowing in the flickering light. His voice was very deep.

"I will sing a powerful song for Warriors about to enter battle with man or spirit." He pulled himself up to his full height and the People knew that here was a man who was fierce.

> Flashing, the blade of my spear is sharp
> to cut holes where none were
> this knife will behead evil
> slash the throats of devils
> around me this leather cloak and shield
> weave a magic pattern
> to confuse and beguile the unwary
> spells are no protection from my power
> I sing a net for evil fish
> now paint the lines on my face
> two lines of the People
> I will go forth to this battle
> with strength in my belly.

After bowing proudly, Yellow Dog sat once more in his place. Echoes of his voice filled the air and Cricket Sings looked to make sure the red lines of war were not actually painted across his cheeks.

Running Water raised a timid hand, then spoke when she realized attention was focused on her. "As you know, I have been a mother most of my life and although some of my children died, two are living and here with us tonight. I would like to sing the lullaby I made for them. It is not a serious song, as were those of One Eye and Yellow Dog, but it is good to calm the little ones as they go home to their beds." She folded her hands across her belly, standing tall in the firelight, a woman at the beginning of old age. Her face was wrinkled, but still plump, and her singing voice was beautiful.

> My little dove
> Sun has traveled to his bed
> soon he will put out his fire
> pull the robes over his dream
> Night is cold for little ones
> here in my arms you will be safe

there are no evils
you are so soft curving to me
I smell the top of your head
my child travel safely
in the journeys of the Night
your hunger is my own
two lights burn in the dark
my eyes watch over you
sleep small love
dream of my arms your cradle
in travels to the stars.

Running Water turned a flushed face to the gathering as she finished her song. Her beloved daughters were smiling in approval and memory.

"You always did know the best song to quiet a fretful baby, sister," praised Cricket Sings. "I think it is time to return to our beds, following Sun's example."

"That is a good idea," replied Running Water. "I, for one, have feasted today and my belly would like to rest and consider its good fortune."

Laughter rippled through the assembled People as they stood, brushed the dust and dry grass from their clothes, and picked up sleeping children. Slowly, they straggled home, calling good night softly between the houses. Cricket Sings sat staring at the fire, trying to divine the future. Wolf Hunter and Doe Eyes settled their children and the apprentice Little One, and the old woman could hear their whispers as they prepared their own bed. The stars were crisp, but far away, and she felt very lonely. Always before the night had been her refuge, a place to be alone. Slowly the great heavens spun, weaving age-old patterns like fine quilling on the robe of sleep. The fire shrank to coals before she heard footsteps coming nearer. Turning her head, she saw the two young Priests following Eagle. As he came into the dim light, she could see that although the young man still wore his Priestly garb, his bearing was full of the power of his new position as Sun in the World.

"Greetings, old woman," he said in a soft, low voice.

"You are indeed Sun in the World," she replied. "The spirit left my visitor while we were attending the Ceremony. It is safe to say that you were the Sun King when you raised the God."

The young man nodded. Cricket Sings waved the two attendants toward the door of her house, anxious to be rid of the danger inside. When they came out, the body was rolled into a robe which sagged between them.

"I thank you, old woman. You have helped me and I am unable to give you anything in return because it might betray our secret. If ever you need a boon, send a message and it will be done."

He turned to leave, but stopped as Cricket Sings motioned him closer.

"There is one matter," she began softly. "Many young women will die to accompany the Sun King into his long Night. I would like my daughter Doe Eyes to be among those who are not chosen for this honor."

He did not answer immediately. When the words came, they were slow and hesitant. "I am not sure of such matters. It may be that the Priests, not I, have the power to choose my father's companions." He knelt beside the old woman sitting on the ground. "Be assured I will do my best to save your daughter should she be chosen."

Before she could reply, he stood and walked into the darkness. Despite the fear in her belly, the old woman felt the heaviness of sleep dragging her body down and she entered the house. In a corner the children slept curled together. Cricket Sings went to her own pallet, where the robes were still curved in the shape of the man who had died there. She bent to smell them. Along with her own scent, she caught a faint musk of death and inhaled deeply. Too soon that would be her own odor. She stretched the robes flat, crawled between them, and fell instantly asleep.

CHAPTER TWELVE
The
Night Flyer

The morning was grey and humid with the promise of rain hanging in the sky. Although Cricket Sings knew the air was not cold, she felt a chill in her belly which could not be comforted. Today the death of the old Sun King and the ascension of Eagle would be formally announced, but it was a good omen that the old Sun King had died on the eve of the Celebration and that his heir had performed the Ceremony with perfection. She rolled onto her side with a moan for the pain in her hips and knees. The younger members of the family slept on, wrapped in dreams.

She woke again and realized that she had been dozing fitfully. Now her bladder was uncomfortably full. She struggled out of the heavy robes, shook herself all over, then stood and walked to the latrine. A few other old women were up and about. Many preferred to sleep late and recover from the excesses of the Celebration. Cricket Sings waved to the other women but did not stop to talk. When she returned to the house she picked up the water bottle and hung it across her back by placing a strap around her forehead. The weight of the bottle was now supported by her neck muscles, strong from many years of carrying burdens. She walked to the lake and set the bottle gently at the edge of the water, then removed her moccasins and waded out until the water rose over her ankles. She stood for a moment, watching the smooth surface of the water, a grey twin to the clouds. At the far side of the pond three ducks were startled by a movement in the bushes and rose in flight like spirits out of the mist. She turned and picked up the spindle-shaped bottle, lowered the mouth to the water and removed the wooden stopper. She held it carefully so that weeds, insects or tiny fish did not enter. When the bottle sank and rested on the lake bottom she knew it was full. She replaced the stopper and stood the bottle upright, pushing the pointed end into the soft sand, then picked it up, shook it slightly to remove some of the wetness and swung it onto her back.

At the water's edge she bent carefully to retrieve her moccasins and walked home barefoot, her calloused feet slapping against the packed dirt. As she passed her fire she noticed a tiny plume of smoke and felt the heat on her shins. There were a few red coals at the very bottom of the fire pit and she set the water bottle into its place near the door before going to the woodpile to search for small sticks with which to cajole the fire into life. Soon she had a roaring blaze and dipped water with her bowl to fill the hot water jug. When the water boiled, she crept quietly into the house so as not to wake her family before they were ready, returning with a tiny bit of yellow flower tea herbs and her comb. She made the tea, then combed her hair, nodding at the white streaks which contrasted with the crow's wing color of her youth. She smoothed the hair across her shoulders, then rebraided it with a sigh for the many times her lover had done this pleasant chore.

As the old woman finished the last braid and reached for her tea bowl, she sensed movement overhead and looked up to see a soundless night flyer landing on the very peak of her roof. Her hand froze in midair. The night flyer turned his impassive face toward her and blinked wide yellow eyes once, then again. Horror jolted through her body as she realized that two of her kind would die. Night flyers did not give false omens.

Cricket Sings felt a wild urge to run through the streets screaming, to tear off her clothes and wail loudly to frighten away the grief which had been foretold. Instead, she pulled her hand back into her lap and folded it inside the other. She tightened every muscle in her body until she felt taut as a bowstring. As though daring the night flyer to take her now, the old woman stared directly at the bird. It remained unaware of her gaze and sat on the roof, swiveling its loose head to survey the area. Cricket Sings thought she would like to take the bird and twist its neck again and again until the head hung limp from its body. She sighed. Even if she killed the bird the omen would remain.

The night flyer moved nervously on the roof, then stretched its wings, flapped them, and took off, swooping low over her. She saw the beauty of its flight, the shaded grey perfection of each wing feather and the tiny ruffs of down above the claws. As suddenly as they had come, the fear and hatred were gone from her body. One could not have evil thoughts about a creature so beautiful. The bird was merely a messenger. Cricket Sings slumped, her muscles sore from the strain.

She reached for her tea at last. It was no longer hot, but the warm liquid was soothing, like a mother's breast to a fretful child. She sucked the tea between her teeth in mouthfuls. Who would die? One Eye perhaps, certainly that old woman was ready for the Long Night. She wondered if she would accompany One Eye. Or would the dead be others of her family or friends? Two of her kind. There were no answers to her questions.

The family began to stir inside the house. As Doe Eyes emerged with Son's wet garments the old woman remained seated at the fire. Doe Eyes did not stop to talk, but went directly to the latrine, rinsing the garments in the stream on her way. When she returned the young woman stretched the wet clothing flat on the thatched roof of the house to dry. Wolf Hunter walked out the door, naked Son in one arm and Daughter giggling in the other. Little One followed. The old woman did not speak. Wolf Hunter did not disturb her, instead pointing the way to the latrine for the apprentice and his daughter. When the younger girl stopped along the path to urinate, he roared her name and she scurried the rest of the way. Son was soon diapered and cuddled in his mother's arms, humming happily as he sucked.

Cricket Sings did not make the porridge, but sat staring at her bare feet. Finally, when Son was full of milk and fast asleep, Doe Eyes handed the baby to his father and made the porridge herself. When it was done cooking she set a bowl at her mother's side to cool. The old woman was startled by the movement and turned her face first to her daughter and then to Wolf Hunter.

"I have to tell you something," she said, pausing before she continued. "There was an evil omen this morning. I have been thinking, but it can have only one meaning. A night flyer perched on top of our house and looked at me. He blinked twice. This means two of my kind will die." She nodded sadly at her own words, then turned tear-filled eyes down to her lap. "We do not know which two," she said softly.

Wolf Hunter and Doe Eyes sat perfectly still. The porridge was cold in the bowls before anyone spoke. At last Wolf Hunter broke the silence.

"You are right that this omen means death; that is the message night flyers bring. But perhaps it will be one death in two days, or two moons."

Cricket Sings shook her head miserably, staring once more into the fire. Daughter brought the family back to life. The two girls had been playing near the edge of the house with sticks and stones and the cornhusk doll Running Water had made. Daughter ran to Doe Eyes, burbling conversation spilling from her lips. When the child saw her mother's sad face she became silent and leaned against Doe Eye's shoulder, laying a tiny hand flat against her mother's cheek. Doe Eyes nuzzled close to the child, accepting her comfort.

"If we don't eat," the young woman said, "Six will die instead of two."

The family returned to the concerns of the living. Cricket Sings picked up the cold bowls of porridge and dumped them back into the cooking pot, adding a little hot water. She stirred the cereal with a stick and placed the pot close to the fire to reheat. Scooping more hot water into her tea bowl, she drank some herself before passing the bowl to Doe Eyes and Wolf Hunter. When the porridge was hot and bubbling once more Doe Eyes went into the house and made mysterious rustling noises inside. Returning with a smile she held out a handful of dried blackberries.

"This is the end of our berries, Sun will have to grow more."

The mood of the family brightened as they mixed the sweet berries into their porridge, watching the purple stain spread through the pale cereal. Little One scooped three fingers of porridge from the bowl into her mouth and smacked her lips.

"This is delicious; you are a woman who can make any occasion happy," Cricket Sings praised her daughter. She continued in a serious voice. "I want you to understand that I have never known a woman who was a better daughter, Doe Eyes. You have been my comfort since your birth."

"Why else does one have children?" replied Doe Eyes sweetly, hugging her own little Daughter closer.

The family rested in the warmth of the fire, enjoying their happiness which might at any moment be shattered. The City came slowly to life. Like sleepy birds twittering in the morning coolness families began to emerge from their houses. Some had food left from the feasting of the day before, others made porridge. Hungry babies squalled while older children climbed trees or played chunky with sticks and stones. Cricket Sings looked up from the fire and saw Soon to be Winter.

"Hello, young Seer," the old woman called out. "Have you had any dreams lately?"

"My good friend, I have come to see you," Soon to be Winter replied. She walked to the fire and gazed into the coals before kneeling next to the old woman. Soon to be Winter laid her smooth hand on Cricket Sings' wrinkled arm. "I have dreamed the end of my life," she said solemnly. "It will come soon now and will be an event of great honor. Dancers paraded through my dream in bright costumes. I flew high above the procession. A great person had died and I was honored with everlasting life to accompany the Holy One. It was a powerful dream!" She nodded her head in agreement with her words.

Cricket Sings was stunned. Despite the rumors, there had been no official announcement of the Sun King's death. Soon to be Winter's knowledge had come from that shadowy beyond out of which souls are born and to which they return after death. The old woman broke the silence.

"Were you young or old as you flew above the procession?"

"Oh, I was the age I am now," Soon to be Winter replied innocently.

Cricket Sings shared a long look with Wolf Hunter. His face was taking on the lines of a much older man. Deep creases now ran from his nose to the corners of his mouth, the result, she knew, of holding fear inside. Carefully, the old woman considered which course of action would prove least dangerous.

"That is a most interesting dream, child," she began. "Have you thought that it might have been inspired by the ceremonies of this time of year rather than by the future?"

"No, I am sure my dream was a prophecy and not merely the wandering of my mind in Night."

Wolf Hunter cleared this throat. "Mother, I must go to the Men's House to speak with my brothers about hunting and other matters of interest to Warriors. Would you like me to inquire about areas abundant in herbs? Perhaps our family might spend a few days camping during this pleasant weather. You would have the help of Doe Eyes and Little One in gathering medicinal plants."

"Camping?" Doe Eyes chimed in. "Oh husband, I would love to see some new country!"

"I think your idea is most intriguing," added Cricket Sings, looking hard at Wolf Hunter. "It is good for People to get out of the City at this time of year. Speak with your brothers about camping places and meanwhile Doe Eyes and I will gather food and put together our tool kits so we can grind corn and sew skins on the trail."

Wolf Hunter nodded. As he stood, Soon to be Winter pushed herself up from her squatting position.

"I am sorry to leave you, my friends," she said. "Cricket Sings, please stop at our house and pick up your knife. Crow Eater has finished splitting the stone and it is the finest work he has ever done."

"I will do that. It will be good to have a sharp new knife to use on this camping trip."

With a wave, Soon to be Winter set off toward the City plaza. It was apparent that she had urgent business, perhaps in regard to her premonition of death. As the dancer reached the road, Cricket Sings allowed a small sigh of relief to escape between her clenched teeth. She spoke directly to Wolf Hunter.

"We must know safe places to go, do you understand?"

Wolf Hunter nodded. "I will learn all I can about the territory to the north, as well as in other directions. We may want to travel first one way, then another, changing if we are followed."

Now it was the old woman's turn to nod and she waved her son-in-law off to do his business. Little One, as a new apprentice, was unperturbed by the currents of worry flowing between the family members. She finished her porridge, licked the bowl clean, then tucked Son's cradleboard into a shady overhang of the house.

Finally, she took Daughter's hand and led the child back to their games.

"Mother," said Doe Eyes softly. Staring into the fire, Cricket Sings did not respond. "Mother," a bit louder. "I am a woman and deserve to know why you speak with my husband in hushed voices, why we had a visitor who appeared and then left in the night, and why now we speak of camping trips at a time when most herbs are still too small for picking."

Cricket Sings did not meet her daughter's eyes. She wanted to keep the young woman sheltered forever from the evils that lay all around. The old woman nodded as she realized that the events of the past few days had made this wish impossible. She looked into Doe Eyes' beautiful face.

"You know of the omen that two of my kind will die, so perhaps there is less need to hide other secrets. There is no one I trust more than you, my daughter, except perhaps your husband. Our visitor was the Sun King."

Doe Eyes gasped. "And he died. . ."

"In our house, but I think he was dead before the Ceremony."

"Who raised the Sun?"

"The heir, young Eagle. He had no choice; the old man was in a sleep from which he would not wake, yet he still lived so that the heir could not publicly assume his role."

Doe Eyes brushed a fly from her cheek with the back of one hand. Her face was grim and strained. "The night flyer and Soon to be Winter's dream are part of your worries about the death of the Sun King. It is clear to me now, Mother, that we should prepare for a journey which might be longer than anyone supposes."

The young woman stood and went into the house. Cricket Sings could hear her rustling in the storage area built into the eaves and knew her daughter was gathering the tool kits. Some tools were too old, others too heavy to carry. In the end they would be able to take only the necessities. The neighbors would think they were going on a short summer camping trip, but the family would travel swiftly and could not be burdened with heavy packs. Doe Eyes appeared in the doorway and the old woman looked up.

"Seed corn, Mother?"

"A very small amount, and some squash and pumpkin seeds, too. I will carry them in my bag."

Doe Eyes returned to her work and Cricket Sings continued to sit by the fire. She was numb and tired from the long vigil of the past few nights. She rocked and hummed her comfort song.

In the distance, a dull booming sound reverberated, repeating regularly. It was the death drum. Doe Eyes must have heard, but she remained at work. The death drum had only one meaning. The Great Sun King had died. There would be no joy in the hearts of the People until he was buried and the heir assumed the role of intercedant with the Gods.

The road was suddenly crowded with People running toward the palisade gate. Carries Stones ran by on his way toward the plaza and called out in excitement. He stopped, breathing heavily, his dirty chest heaving.

"Honored Woman, are you not going to see the Priests?"

"I know the meaning of that drum; it called the People when I was young. My son-in-law has gone to hear the news."

Carries Stones resumed running toward the gate. The old woman heard feet scrambling behind her and turned to see Wolf Hunter, breathless and pale, approaching the house.

"It is true, the Sun King is dead," he said. "I have come to tell you this news so that we might be among the first to honor the dead with mourning."

Doe Eyes appeared in the doorway of the house. She let out a loud wail of anguish, bent to pick up a handful of dust and threw it over her head. "Auugh," she cried. "The Sun King is dead. Restless spirits prowl and I must protect myself."

Wolf Hunter followed his wife's example and began to scream and throw dust. Cricket Sings walked to the water jug at the door, scooped a gourd dipper full and splashed water on the ground next to the house. When she had thoroughly wetted the earth the old woman bent and stirred the mixture with her hand. The mud was thin but sticky and she painted her face to show that death was in her soul as well as in the World. Continuing their mourning cries, Wolf Hunter and Doe Eyes approached the mud puddle and smeared any skin not covered by clothing with mud. As Daughter and Little One rounded the corner of the house they were immediately covered with mud by the adults. Doe Eyes went to her small Son, sleeping in the shady corner near the door, and blackened his cheeks.

From surrounding houses similar cries could be heard and soon the entire City was filled with shrieking, mud-covered mourners. Women threw themselves against trees, their faces and arms cut and bleeding from the sharp bark. Others whirled around in the dusty street until they became dizzy and fell to the ground. As the People had become One in celebration, so they were now One in sorrow. The mourners forgot work, hunger, all the routines of life as they became caught up in waves of grief.

Cricket Sings began her own death song, shuffling her bare feet in the dust, making a small circular path. After each step she reached down for a pinch of dust to throw in the air. When Doe Eyes and Wolf Hunter saw what she was doing they began their own circles, singing death songs only partially formed because of their youth. The People sang to lift the Sun King to his place with the other Gods. It was a holy duty. Until the Sun King presented his heir to the Gods the People were cut off from the spirit world. So the People danced, building a boat of song for the Sun King's long journey home.

CHAPTER THIRTEEN
Brides are Chosen

When the Sun rose high the first frenzy of mourning had passed, and the People began to provide themselves with the necessities of life while maintaining public grieving. Son was the first to rebel, announcing his hunger with angry cries. Doe Eyes hurried to calm him. Sitting with her back against the side of the house she pulled the cradleboard across her lap and bent slightly so that the child could take hold of her breast. She winced as the baby bit hard, but then he settled down to rhythmic sucking, choking back a few last hiccoughing sobs between mouthfuls of milk. Doe Eyes held her Son close, rocking him in the rhythm of her heart, but still she sang the mourning songs.

Cricket Sings was tired. Although she walked long distances each day her knees wobbled now, and she began to stumble and fall in the dance. Finally she had to rest, squatting near the fire and singing in time with Doe Eyes. Wolf Hunter and the two girls, Little One and Daughter, continued the dance, making circles in the dust while Sun climbed.

After Son finished his meal and let out a healthy burp, Doe Eyes went into the house and returned with her mano, metate and a small bag of corn. She knelt before the metate, breaking the corn with the pressure of the paired stones. Back and forth she swayed, rubbing the corn until the pieces were very fine. In rhythm with the mourning voices she rose, walked to the woodpile and chose three small logs to replenish the fire. With a stick she moved coals next to the flat baking stone so it would heat. Then she began to make the breads for their meal, scooping the ground corn into a shallow bowl and adding just the right amount of cool water to make a paste. She squatted next to her mother and began patting a handful of dough into a flat, round bread. She placed a round of dough on the stone, forming a second while the first one baked. The old woman broke off her song as the first bread turned golden brown. Sliding it carefully onto her hand, Cricket Sings flipped it over and broke off the crisp edges to eat first. When she was finished she did not relax and make tea as usual. Instead, she rose and motioned to Wolf Hunter that it was his turn to eat. She assumed his place, letting out great howls to notify the Gods of her presence.

Stirred by thousands of feet, fine dust rose from the streets of the City and mixed with sweat, sticking to every inch of skin. By late afternoon Cricket Sings was numb with exhaustion, but still she took her turns dancing. Little One and Daughter slept inside the house during the hottest part of the day. As the afternoon wore on, two danced and one rested, with Wolf Hunter and Doe Eyes taking longer turns so the old woman could rest.

All the People were tired. Up and down the road they danced before their houses. The heavy drum had stopped when Sun reached his highest point, but now began its call anew. One delegate from each family was chosen to go to the plaza to get the seeds. For this one Night all the People would know the dreams and visions of the Priests. Wolf Hunter stopped dancing when they heard the renewed booming of the great drum. He looked at his wife, then at Cricket Sings. The old woman nodded. Without speaking it was decided that he should go. Crow Eater was passing, and Wolf Hunter broke the mourning by calling the other young man's name, then hurried to catch up when Crow Eater waved.

After the two men were out of sight, Cricket Sings and Doe Eyes both slumped to rest beside the fire. A few breads lay beside the cooking stone, dry and unappetizing. The old woman absentmindedly munched on a broken chip of corn bread, then called Little One and Daughter, who had wakened from their nap, and gave each girl a piece. Daughter began a burbling laugh, but was cut off as her grandmother placed a hand over her mouth.

"Silence, child," the old woman hissed. "This is a time for mourning, not for joy. Your happiness will be rewarded with death should the Priests catch you smiling. Remember!"

The old woman held the astonished child by the shoulder and shook her once, then again. Daughter cried softly, sniffling when her nose began to run. Little One walked to the smaller girl, took her by the hand, and led her to the back of the house where a solemn group of children had gathered. They did not play, sitting instead in a circle. The old woman could hear the children humming fragments of the mourning songs they had heard the adults sing.

"Mother," Doe Eyes began.

"Do not tell me that I was cruel," Cricket Sings cut her off. "I know, I know I have never frightened her before, but it is better to be cruel than to have the child dead because she rejoiced at the death of the Sun King."

Doe Eyes nodded. "What will happen now?" she asked. "You saw the death of a King when you were young."

"I am not sure, for customs change as young Priests replace the old men. But the drum called the People to the Holy Hill to receive a ration of the seeds with which the Priests induce visions. Tonight the People will share the hidden facets of their souls." She shuddered. "It is like taking a fine knife and turning it inside out so that the inner surfaces of the stone are exposed. Once, I experienced such ecstasy, and it was as though I would die forever. I do not want the seeds again."

The old woman straightened as she said these last words. She placed her small strong hands on her knees and pushed herself to a standing position, then stretched and grimaced as the knotted muscles in her back pulled and loosened.

"Keep the children in the house for this day and night. I cannot say what evil things will be loosed on the City. Some of the People will die in this terror."

"But if the seeds provide beautiful visions we have nothing to fear," Doe Eyes replied.

Before she had finished speaking her mother whirled and, with eyes flashing, walked to Doe Eyes and slapped her face. The young woman did not move. Tears gathered in her eyes. Cricket Sings spoke quietly but distinctly.

"You are the one I love above all others, yet I hurt you. Think of what I said. These seeds can be beautiful, but they are a lie, turning at any moment to blackest nightmare. You cannot imagine the horrors you will see this Night. If you were to eat the seeds you would always be another person, half of you remaining in that world inside where everything is strange."

Cricket Sings turned away and sat silently beside the fire. She felt her back slump and drew her knees up to her chest, resting her head on top of them. Doe Eyes called Little One and Daughter to her side.

"Little One," she said. "I know that you are new in our house, but I need your help. Those who have passed the age of knowledge will eat the seeds; it is the law of the People. We ascend with the Sun King into the regions of the Gods. I fear for my children."

Little One nodded. "I will keep the children in the house. Daughter and I will play and your Son is a good baby."

Doe Eyes reached a gentle hand toward Little One. At first the girl flinched from the contact, but then she leaned closer and allowed her cheek to be stroked for a moment before she turned and ran behind the house.

Doe Eyes sighed and went into the house, returning with a few pieces of dried fish, a handful of corn and some tubers which grew on the roots of the tall man plants in the marsh. To the west, clouds were building, but overhead the sky was a brilliant blue. She went to the fire and set a bowl near the hottest coals. After adding several small sticks to start a hot cooking fire, she dipped water into the bowl to heat and added the fish, corn and tubers. When the soup came to a boil she scraped away all but a few coals from the base of the bowl. The mixture would steam and make a rich broth.

Cricket Sings remained seated at the fireside, her head hanging down. Slow spirals of smoke rose from the fires of the City, but the usual noises of gossiping adults and playing children had been replaced by a strange quiet. Doe Eyes began to doze in the sunlight, sitting upright, her head jerking when she fell too deeply asleep.

The old woman stood suddenly and walked away toward the house of Running Water. She sorrowed that at this most dangerous time she had struck her daughter, yet she knew there was sometimes no other way to teach. Her daughter would remember that eating the seeds was a serious matter, not a game for idle children. She noticed the quiet of the City. Mothers kept their children beside the home fire. Many women were preparing soup, which would be eaten at any hour of the night. She passed between two houses, waving in answer to a soft greeting called by a thin woman who was big with child. The old woman quickened her pace. She wanted to stop her sister from eating the seeds. Since the experience of her youth she had avoided contact with any material which might induce ghostly visions.

There was no fire in front of Running Water's house. It appeared deserted, but when Cricket Sings flipped the doormat back and peered inside she saw her sister lying on a bed of skins in the far corner. Running Water looked up with swollen eyes.

"The have taken my daughters," she whispered hoarsely.

Cricket Sings felt fear stab into her belly. She held onto the doorway to keep herself from falling.

"After the men left, the Priests came looking, and my neighbor . . ." the plump woman's voice broke. She sobbed once, then continued in a shaky voice. ". . . my neighbor, who has always been jealous of our good fortune, pointed out our house. I had the girls well hidden in the grain storage pit, but the Priests came right into the house and took them by the arm. I was so afraid I did not know what to do." She began to cry with deep, choking sobs.

Cricket Sings felt the horror seeping through her. She had not thought the holy ones would be chosen so soon. It appeared that the Priests would hurry those dark ceremonies surrounding the disposal of the dead Sun King's body. She knelt beside the sobbing woman, circling her with a trembling arm.

"They were my last two children," Running Water cried softly into her sister's boney shoulder. "I am old now and will never have more. There will be no fat grandchildren to roll in the dust at my fire. I will die alone and my stories will end."

Cricket Sings rocked her sister in her arms, singing the mourning song. Together the women wailed, forgetting the greater sorrow of the People for their dead King. A new Sun King would rule, but there would be no new daughters for Running Water.

The scuffling of moccasined feet caused the old woman to sit upright. Someone was waiting outside the house. It could not be a family member, for one of their own would have called out a greeting. This person was a stranger. She pressed a firm hand over Running Water's mouth to quiet her questions.

"Shh, sister, wait here. I heard a footstep outside and I am going to see who is waiting so silently."

Running Water nodded, stifled her grief, and sat up. She picked up her comb and began to unbraid her hair. Her plump body was shaken by silent sobs, but no sound escaped her lips. Cricket Sings stood and left the house, squinted as the late Sun dazzled her.

"Hello, old woman," said the soft voice of Touch the Hawk. "I came to see if Night Bird was here, or her mother, for I wish to take her in marriage. I have trading to do and must travel south after this sad occasion."

When the old woman did not speak he walked to her, took a wrinkled hand in his smooth young one and led her to the fireplace. He motioned for Cricket Sings to sit. She did as he wished. Touch the Hawk went to the woodpile and returned with several small sticks of kindling. In the ritual of the People, he renewed the fire and when at last a small blaze was crackling he sat beside Cricket Sings. She spoke.

"Night Bird will never be your bride. The Priests have taken the sisters to accompany the dead Sun King into Night."

Touch the Hawk held up his hand. There was no need to say more. His face, which had been cheerful, became smooth and hid his feelings. A rustling came from the door of the house and Cricket Sings turned to see her sister. Running Water had always been light of foot, despite the considerable bulk of her body. Now she moved like an old woman, slowly and with pain. Her eyes were swollen nearly shut from crying, and although her hair was neatly braided it fell across her shoulders without life. Cricket Sings suddenly wondered if her sister would die of grief. Running Water made her way to the fire and sat beside the young man who would have been her son-in-law. Then she spoke, with effort but with great dignity.

"I heard your reason for being here and I thank you for courting Night Bird. She was happy during the Celebration because of your presence in our family. You would have been a good son."

Tears welled from her eyes and ran down her cheeks, falling into her lap unnoticed. There was a long silence before Touch the Hawk spoke in a hard, low voice.

"I think we cannot allow this to happen. Young girls should not be killed to accompany an old man. We can find where they are keeping your daughters and steal them away from the Priests. In my travels I have come to know all the trails of the People, and also those beyond the reach of the Sun King's power. We could live by ourselves, without the City."

Touch the Hawk was very intense and his soft eyes were gleaming. The gentle young man had disappeared and even his twisted back seemed straighter.

"I am a Warrior by birth and training, although this evil in my back has prevented me from assuming my full station. I can hunt, and Night Bird can learn about herbs and roots and dry berries and fish. We will survive."

"We had already planned an escape in case the Priests came for Doe Eyes," the herb woman answered slowly.

"I will go," said Running Water.

Cricket Sings looked at her sister. The sagging lines in Running Water's face firmed as her resolve grew.

"I will go, and Starving Creek will accompany us. He will not like to leave his old mother who has no one to hunt for her, but she can have this house and there are many copper ornaments to sell for food." Running Water stood. "Go find Starving Creek and bring him to me. We will talk and make a plan. The Priests said the brides will be kept on the Holy Hill in a small hut. Tonight they will be given the seeds like the rest of the People. If we do not eat the seeds, the others may be too confused to know what we are doing." Running Water placed her hand on Touch the Hawk's shoulder. "Perhaps I will have grandchildren yet. Now I will prepare our tool kits. It would be good to carry food for several days, but perhaps we will travel too slowly with such heavy burdens. I will make one pack with tools and two more with food."

Running Water turned toward her house and began to make busy noises inside. Cricket Sings remained at the fire with Touch the Hawk, looking after her sister in amazement. For the first time in her life Running Water was not babbling foolishly. The herb woman spoke hesitantly.

"I cannot speak for the rest of my family. We worried that the Priests might take married women, that my own daughter Doe

Eyes would be in danger, and made secret plans to escape at any moment. We did not think the Priests would act so soon. Doe Eyes is preparing packs with tool kits and food. Wolf Hunter went to the Men's House to speak with his brothers about trails and game. Like you, Yellow Dog is a trader and had plans to leave the City after the Celebration. It may be that we should travel together."

"Where are Yellow Dog and Wolf Hunter now?"

"I do not know about Yellow Dog. Wolf Hunter went to get our ration of seeds so he would not appear to be acting suspiciously and thus draw attention to our trip."

"It is almost dusk. Find Wolf Hunter or Yellow Dog and ask them to meet me here at dark. Do not have the women come here. I will send Running Water to your house." He spoke in a louder voice for the neighbors to hear. "Has Starving Creek gone to fetch the seeds for your family?"

"Yes," replied Running Water, her voice muffled by the walls of the house.

Touch the Hawk stood and spoke softly. "The men will meet here at dark. Caution them not to eat even a few of those seeds or they will be useless to us this night." He stretched. His body was twisted, but the muscles moved powerfully beneath his skin and his chest was wide and smooth.

"We will wait for you in the Night," said Cricket Sings.

"Yes," he answered. "In the Night."

He walked toward the palisade gate. Dusk was creeping in around the corners of the houses and beneath trees. The clouds were now enormous, piled high in the west. Behind them Sun was invisible. Cricket Sings picked up a twig and dug a small track in the powdery dirt in front of her, then stood and threw the twig into the fire, thinking of the long trip ahead. She brushed her dress carefully.

"Sister, I am going home now," she called softly.

Running Water appeared at the door of the house, a large flat carrying basket in her hands. "I heard what Touch the Hawk said about going to your house, Cricket Sings. I will ready three packs and carry one with me."

"No, leave the packs in a corner of your house, covered with robes to look like a bed. Be sure to wear warm clothes because when winter comes we may not have a house."

"You are right. As soon as I have finished here I will walk to your fire."

"Good. Doe Eyes has made a soup. We will sit by the fire and pretend to eat the seeds."

Cricket Sings turned to walk home. Running Water spoke quietly to her back.

"Sister, do you think we will save my children?"

The older woman turned back, but she did not step closer. For an instant she considered telling Running Water about the night flyer, but decided it would be wiser to keep such worries to herself.

"I think the men will do their best," she said. "They have great power, and it may be that they will succeed. I will await your presence at my fire."

She turned and began walking away swiftly so that Running Water would not see the fear in her eyes. A few very holy families were continuing their mourning dances. Soon to be Winter was on the road and waved, breaking into a trot. She was breathless when she stopped in front of Cricket Sings.

"Hello, my old friend. I am on my way to give myself as a bride for the dead Sun King," she said in a rapturous voice. Her eyes looked wild, showing white all around the dark centers. "When the drums began I knew my fate. The Priests have so far taken only maidens, but I am young and pretty and my fine dancing will entertain the Sun King in his long Night." She danced a little circle in front of Cricket Sings to demonstrate.

The old woman shook her head and stared at her friend, eyes wide in amazement. "Have you lost your senses? You are going to offer yourself for death? Child, child, think again! You have a good husband who treats you well, and a role to fulfill as a Seer for the People. Many children will come from your body."

"Oh, none of this matters," said the young woman, waving her hands as though to push such ideas out of the way. "At my house Crow Eater sits by the fire crying like a child. He should be honored that his wife was chosen by the Gods, but instead he tried to hold me back and begged me to stay with him. He does not understand! Why would I want to be the wife of a stone worker when I can live forever with the Sun King?"

Before Cricket Sings could stop her, the Seer hurried down the road toward the plaza. The old woman looked after her. Soon to be Winter was beautiful, with shining hair and eyes. Even though she was married, the Priests would certainly accept her as a concubine. The greatest Seers always had a craziness in their thoughts. The excitement of the festival combined with the death of the Sun King and the strange dream had clouded Soon to be Winter's mind. She would never be content until she joined the Sun King in death. The old woman turned toward her home, hunching her shoulders against the evil which now hovered so near.

CHAPTER FOURTEEN
The Plan

Doe Eyes was sitting at the fireside with Son on her lap. The empty cradleboard lay on the ground. Little One cuddled Daughter next to Doe Eyes. When Cricket Sings approached them without a word Doe Eyes spoke.

"My husband has not returned. I think he has been making plans."

"Are the tool kits ready, and the packs with food?"

"Yes."

"Good." Cricket Sings hesitated, then spoke in a flat voice. "The Sun Priests have taken Running Water's children."

"My cousins?" Doe Eyes turned a horror-stricken face up to her mother.

"Yes. Touch the Hawk is looking for your husband, as well as Yellow Dog and Starving Creek. There is a plan to get the girls back and go on a long trip. Touch the Hawk and Yellow Dog know trails from trading and your husband has spoken with his brothers about a hunting trip. No one will know for sure where we have gone. The important thing is not to eat the seeds, for we must be in possession of our souls tonight."

Cricket Sings looked directly at her daughter and felt her eyes fill with tears. "I am sorry," she whispered as the tears overflowed. "I never meant to hurt you, only to keep you from harm."

Doe Eyes reached out a hand to her mother, who took it gladly.

"I know, old woman, I understand. These times are difficult."

"That is no excuse for anger toward those you love."

"You cannot expect to be without fault."

They heard the whisper of moccasins on the road and turned to see who was walking toward their house. It was Yellow Dog, and he looked very strange. He was not walking upright, but instead leaned to one side. The old Warrior's legs seemed to be mixed up, and he was tripping and weaving from side to side on the road. He lifted a hand in greeting and stumbled slowly toward them.

"Oh oh, he has eaten the seeds already," said Cricket Sings in a voice just loud enough for Doe Eyes to hear. "He will be of no use to us tonight. Keep our plans secret. Yellow Dog will have no control over his tongue." She called out to the old man. "Hello, cousin, how goes your day?"

Yellow Dog seemed not to see or hear. He continued on his way, walking past the women and stepping into the center of the fire. He did not appear to be burned and continued through the fire pit, breaking two pots and narrowly missing the soup pot. Walking straight to a tree at the south side of the house, Yellow Dog clasped it and murmured into the bark. He appeared to be delirious.

"I should not have counted on that one; he is too fond of other Worlds to remain behind when they are freely offered by the Priests," the old woman muttered.

"Oh, my little tree, my sweet bride," crooned Yellow Dog, rubbing himself vigorously up and down against the bark and tearing the decorative quilling from his shirt.

"His wife will not be happy that he is ruining her fine sewing," answered Doe Eyes.

"She will eat the seeds herself and forget such matters in her encounter with the Gods."

"Mother, do you think Wolf Hunter will eat the seeds?"

"It is a difficult thing to avoid because the Priests give a packet of seeds to each man and then invite him to partake of a few for the journey home. Perhaps Wolf Hunter will try to delay by saying he wishes to share the seeds with his family. We will hope he is strong enough to stare into the eyes of Priests and lie."

"Look, Mother!" cried Doe Eyes, pointing toward the road.

A group of men and women were staggering in the dust, tiny bags of seeds clutched in their hands. They walked with the same crazy gait as Yellow Dog, catching hold of each other to keep from falling. Three collapsed suddenly in a heap, laughing and rolling as though bathing in the dirt.

"They all seem to be having a good time," observed Doe Eyes as she began to straighten the fireplace, using a stick to push the coals back into the firepit.

"Yes, at first the seeds are very happy, but as Night comes the pleasant dreams will turn to terror. Ugly spirits are gathering, and the People, including our Yellow Dog so busy now making love to that tree, will scream and run in fear. It is better that the children stay hidden in the house tonight."

Doe Eyes stood and handed Son to Cricket Sings. She picked up the shards of broken pottery and tossed them to one side of the fire. The grandmother held the baby close to her sagging bosom and rocked in an ancient rhythm.

"Little One, Daughter," called Doe Eyes loudly. "It is time to eat and make your bed. Strange spirits walk the City and it is better for children to be sheltered from ghosts."

She held out a hand to each girl and the children came obediently. Doe Eyes led them to the fire.

"I have two hungry and very dirty girls all ready for soup."

The three sat down near Cricket Sings.

Yellow Dog was now groveling at the the foot of the tree. "Please, my sweetheart, my wife is no longer happy with me. She will place my moccasins and bow outside the door and then I will come to live in your green arms." Streaked with sweat and dust, Yellow Dog looked up at the tree.

Cricket Sings snorted in disgust.

"Yellow Dog is no longer in our World," Doe Eyes agreed.

"Soon the tree will turn on Yellow Dog and become a devil. His screaming and wailing will be most unpleasant when the devils come. Ah, here is my sister."

"What's wrong with him?" asked Running Water, gesturing toward Yellow Dog with a disgusted look on her face.

"He has eaten the seeds and now walks with spirits, but his choice of company was not wise. He has developed a great passion for that tree, and she does not fancy him a proper lover."

Running Water sat next to Daughter and crossed her legs. "I thought as much. He will be of no use to us tonight."

"We will not take Yellow Dog on our trip," suggested the herb woman. "Soon he will be howling, and noise does not make a safe journey."

Running Water nodded and held out her arms for Son. Her eyes were still swollen but she had regained her hopeful spirits.

"Little boy, little boy," she sang softly into the baby's ear. "I once had a fat little Son like you." Turning to her sister, Running Water asked, "When can we expect to see the men? I am worried about waiting too long. Everyone will have eaten the seeds."

"I do not think we need to worry much about being noticed," answered Cricket Sings. "Yellow Dog has not even seen us sitting here."

"Yes," agreed Running Water as her face broke into a smile. "But he is young again and in love with a beautiful spirit. Everyone knows a man in love has eyes for no one but his sweetheart."

"Oowoo," cried Yellow Dog. He was now lying on the ground at the foot of the tree. "You are heartless. What can I do to please you? Would you like a fine house, robes to cover your branches from the winter snows? Shall I find a bird's nest to adorn your hair?"

"At least the old man is offering gifts appropriate for a tree," said Doe Eyes. "Does everyone act this way after eating the seeds?"

"You saw that group in the road; they must be at the same stage as our old cousin," the herb woman answered. "Depending on how many seeds were eaten, sooner or later the visions turn to terror. When this becomes frenzy, the worshipper is very near to death."

"In our youth a Sun King died," added Running Water. "Cricket Sings and I were old enough to eat the seeds, but we delayed. Our neighbor climbed a tree and tried to fly like a bird. He was killed. The seeds make the spirit soar, but the body remains in this World. Perhaps the man flew, but we saw him lying broken on the ground just before Grandmother made us eat our seeds."

Little One and Daughter sat wide-eyed as Doe Eyes dipped them each a bowl of soup. Cricket Sings' nose twitched at the delicious odor. The little girls drank the liquid from their bowls, then used their fingers to eat tender morsels of fish and vegetables.

"Good Mama, good Sings!" said Daughter.

"I will have a bowl of that soup," said Cricket Sings as she stood. "Sister, how about you?"

"My appetite is not good since my daughters were taken."

"Nonetheless, you must eat. You need strength to get them safely out of the City tonight."

The old woman walked to the house, stepped inside, and returned with three bowls. She filled one for Running Water, then Doe Eyes and finally herself. The women slurped the liquid, using their fingers to eat the solid bits at the bottom of the bowls.

"What about him?" asked Doe Eyes, nodding toward Yellow Dog.

"Ah, leave the silly old man alone. He will not eat, the spirits do not care about food." Cricket Sings smacked her lips.

The other two women laughed harshly and finished their soup; then they settled around the fire to wait for dusk. A shriek came from the neighbor's house. As the shadows stretched longer the ugly spirit World grew more and more powerful until the air was filled with strange vibrations, the coming and going of unseen creatures. Cricket Sings grew restless and turned to Running Water.

"The men are to meet at your house at dark?"

"That is my understanding. They will decide how to rescue my daughters."

"I am tired of sitting here waiting for those men to do something. If we leave now we can walk to your house and meet them. If they do not need our help we will bring back the tools and food."

"Mother," reminded Doe Eyes gently. "There are some things in which old women should not meddle, including weapons and fighting."

Cricket Sings looked hard at her daughter before she answered. "My weapon is my wits. I will use them to get those girls off the Holy Hill. There will be many young women up there by now, all crazy from the seeds. It will be difficult to steal my nieces without causing alarm."

"I have an idea," Running Water interrupted. "We could take beautiful garments up the hill and tell the Priests that my daughters must have their fine clothes to look their best when they accompany the Sun King. Will the Priests be crazy, too?"

"Priests often eat the seeds. They are better able to remember the real World than People who are not used to such contact with the spirits. Perhaps they will question us, but your trick is worth trying. Who would suspect two old women, faithful handmaidens of the Sun?"

"What about me?" asked Doe Eyes.

"You have the most important role. It is necessary that you remain here and be crazy to represent our family. Every household must take the seeds so the Priests can see their faith."

"But I have no seeds, Mother."

"No, no, no. The idea is not to eat the seeds, but to appear as if you have. Put on your oldest dress, rip it, smear yourself with dirt and watch carefully to see what the others do. Especially him." Cricket Sings gestured toward Yellow Dog, who was grappling with invisible devils.

Doe Eyes rose from her seat by the fire. Son was asleep in Running Water's arms. The baby did not wake as his mother lifted him gently from his aunt's arms and carried him into the house. When Son was safely tucked into a pile of robes, Doe Eyes returned.

"I am going to have Little One keep the children in the house. Your advice about acting crazy is good and I will do my best, but there is one problem. With you as my example I have been dignified for so many years that it may be very difficult to be crazy." With a nervous giggle, Doe Eyes took the two little girls into the house.

"That one has no respect for her mother," said Cricket Sings.

"On the contrary, I think she honors you," answered her sister. "Forget about respect, we have work to do." Running Water stood. "It is nearly dark."

Cricket Sings rose and shook herself to loosen the stiff places. Long shadows stretched over the City as the two old women set off together. The People were in varying stages of entrancement. Some sat quietly next to cold fireplaces, looking into the ashes as though a fire still burned. One usually dignified elder was rolling in a mud hole, whooping in glee. A couple was engaged in love-making openly in the street. Running Water poked her sister with her elbow.

"Look, she is not even that one's wife!"

"This is a disgrace," said Cricket Sings. "The People have forgotten the ancient power which held them to the right path. That mother is holding her baby up by the feet! I must do something!"

She stepped off the road as though to rescue the child, but Running Water grabbed her arm.

"We have no time for that now. Our need is elsewhere."

"You are right. The fire must be out at your house, I do not see any smoke."

"Do you see the men?"

"No, but there are two Priests approaching. They are checking to see whether the People are enjoying their seeds. I think we should hide, perhaps they have not seen us."

The women ducked behind a tree and wiggled into the brambles surrounding the base. The herb woman cursed under her breath.

"I do not like these stickers. Why did you have to choose this tree?"

"Shh."

Cricket Sings peered out from under a briar directly into the eyes of one of the young Priests she had seen on the Holy Hill the night of the feast. He did not appear to see her. His eyes were very liquid and wide, gazing into the other World. The Priests passed in a measured pace, walking in time to unheard drums. Just past the tree the younger man stopped suddenly and put out an arm to stop his companion in the same place. He carefully picked up a stick from the side of the road and felt in the dust, lifting the stick into the air as though flipping an invisible snake off the tip. Then he jumped straight up, coming down with both feet on the exact spot where the invisible snake had landed. With the snake dead, the Priests continued their course down the road, checking every few steps to make sure no evil omens lay in their path. When they were out of sight Cricket Sings sighed with relief and turned to her sister.

"I was afraid they would see us. That one looked straight at me, and he knows who I am."

"I did not know you knew any of the Priesthood."

"I was called to treat the illness of a Priest recently and that one helped to carry the patient," the herb woman lied.

"Listen, do you hear anything from the road?"

"No. It is very dark; we will have to hurry."

Cricket Sings crawled out of the bushes and turned to pull her sister by the arm.

"Wait, wait, you are ripping the flesh off my legs," the plump woman whispered loudly.

When Running Water crawled out of the bushes her legs were covered with long bleeding welts where the thorns had caught and held her. A red line trickled down one ankle and she brushed it with her hand, smearing blood across her leg.

"Soon we will look as though we really had eaten the seeds," she said, panting. "I am getting too old for these games. Next year perhaps we will have a quieter Celebration. Look, there is Wolf Hunter."

The herb woman squinted and saw Wolf Hunter look over his shoulder as he slipped through the door. When the women neared the house they could hear the low murmur of male voices inside. Running Water hurried the last few steps, flipped back the doorskin and ducked inside. The men stopped their talk. Wolf Hunter grabbed the plump woman by the arm and pulled her to a place beside him on the floor, then gestured to Cricket Sings, who pushed the doorskin into place behind her.

Four men were sitting around the cold fireplace. Touch the Hawk and Starving Creek were expected, but the fourth man was Crow Eater. Cricket Sings blinked in surprise.

"What are you doing here?" she asked.

"My wife is crazy. She had not even eaten the seeds when she went to the Holy Hill to offer herself to the God. I want her back." Crow Eater lifted his hands and shrugged.

"Never mind how he got here, woman, we are making a plan," growled Starving Creek impatiently.

Cricket Sings folded her overdress around her hips and sat carefully on the floor next to Touch the Hawk.

"We already have a plan," said Running Water as she stood and walked to the rear of the house. She rummaged in the overhead storage area as the herb woman spoke to the men.

"My sister has an idea to get inside the hut where the girls are waiting. They have probably been given many seeds and are knowing both beautiful visions and devils. The back of the hut will be at the north side of the hill, not far from the creek. Running Water and I will pester the Priests. We will carry fine garments for the girls to wear, for they would not want to wed the God in everyday clothes."

The men listened quietly.

"That is good so far, old woman, but what will you do next?" asked Touch the Hawk.

"We will get inside the hut and talk to the girls. We can tell them we are Priests disguised as women, that we have been sent to take them to the God." Cricket Sings turned to Crow Eater. "Do not worry, we will do the same for Soon to be Winter. She is my sister in spirit." The old woman turned back and continued. "We will loosen a hole in the wall at the rear of the hut. From there we can slide down the side of the hill, pushing the girls ahead of us. They will be crazy, but if we caution them that this is all part of the wedding they may listen and obey. You men will be hiding at the bottom of the hill, ready to guide us to the boats where Doe Eyes and the children will be hidden."

Wolf Hunter's face was grim, and Starving Creek drew his mouth into a thin line. There was a long silence before Touch the Hawk turned to the old woman.

"You two have made a good plan. See," he turned to the other men, "I told you grandmothers are good for something."

They all laughed in relief. Running Water picked up an armful of beautifully decorated ceremonial garments.

"Do you think these will get us past the Priests?" she asked, holding up a dress embroidered with quilling at the neck and hem.

"Let's begin this journey we are making," said Starving Creek, jumping to his feet. His long thin arms were trembling with excitement.

"Wait!" Cricket Sings remained seated and waved her hand to hold back the men. "I think we should talk about the long trip. Doe Eyes has prepared small packs with tool kits and food. Running Water has done likewise." She gestured toward the corner where the three packs were piled together. "How will we carry these things to the meeting place? Where are the boats hidden? Remember, Doe Eyes will have the help of Little One with the babies."

"What about Yellow Dog and his family?" asked Wolf Hunter.

Cricket Sings made her mouth wet and spat into the empty fireplace. "That one could not wait to eat the seeds. I knew there was a reason his father named him after a dog. He is garbage."

Touch the Hawk broke the silence. "I have an idea. Three men will carry the packs to my boat. You women walk slowly to the Holy Hill and begin your trickery. Wolf Hunter can bring Doe Eyes and the children to the boats and hide them in the bushes, then join us at the base of the hill."

Everyone nodded.

"We are agreed, then," he said. "Old women, we will see you at the bottom of the hill." He turned to the men. "Go silently."

Three shadows of men disappeared like mist between the houses. Wolf Hunter walked to the road and began to stumble toward home in imitation of the drunken gait of the seed eaters.

CHAPTER FIFTEEN
On The Holy Hill

Cricket Sings stood in the doorway, watching as Wolf Hunter got smaller and smaller until the Night swallowed him. She jumped when her sister spoke.

"We should carry these dresses with all the decorations showing so the Priests can see we are serious about clothing my daughters in their finest."

The two women began to sort through the dresses, folding and piling them neatly.

"I would like a cup of yellow flower tea," muttered the herb woman.

"I am sorry that I have nothing to offer you."

"If I were wise and carried my medicine bag with me there would be no reason not to have tea."

"Will Wolf Hunter remember to bring your medicine bag to the meeting place?"

"Doe Eyes will carry the bag. She is my daughter."

Running Water nodded and stood, laying the dresses neatly over her arm. Cricket Sings pushed herself to her feet and shook her overdress into position so that it hung smoothly from her shoulders. She sighed.

"We are ready," she said.

They walked toward the palisade gate at a dignified pace, skirting revelers in the road. The City was always busy, but on this

Night the usually purposeful activity had become wild. Running Water walked faster and the older woman grew tired.

"Sister!" she called out. "Sister, wait, my legs are stiff."

Running Water looked back and stopped to wait at the opening in the palisade. The sisters entered the gate together, then passed through the holy space between the twin death mounds of the Priests. Cricket Sings felt the now-familiar evil hovering nearby.

"I do not like this place. Bad things happen here, spirits are waiting to catch us in the Night."

"Shh," hissed her sister. "We must pretend to be crazy like the others."

The herb woman did not answer, instead putting her arm through her sister's so that they were linked together into one clumsy creature. Running Water copied her sister's wavering gait and together they lurched toward the plaza. As they reached the open area the women avoided the People who had gathered in small groups. Two children were wandering in circles, crying for their mother.

"A sad thing." The old woman gestured toward the lost ones with her free arm. "I suppose their mother is either dead or consorting with evil. Those children will not see morning. Someone will tire of their crying and knock them on the head."

As the women passed the market of the herb sellers, Cricket Sings looked for One Eye, but her tent had vanished. They entered the avenue leading to the Holy Hill. Three Priests were huddled at the approach to the mound, heads close together. Cricket Sings felt Running Water pull backward, but dragged her reluctant sister boldly ahead toward the men.

"Good evening, my fine fellows! Which of you has the higher rank? We need to speak with someone of very high rank." She made her voice loud.

One Priest stepped foward. Tall for a man of the People, he had a wide chest and powerful arms. He wore a breechcloth as well as the quilled badge of his office. All three had slicked their hair back with grease and secured it with hairpins carved of bone.

"I am in charge here," the young Priest said in a surprisingly high clear voice.

He had the wide-eyed look which came after eating many seeds.

"Our daughters have been chosen as brides of the dead King. When the Priests took the girls there was no time to change to festive garments. We know they should be dressed properly for a wedding, so we brought these beautiful clothes." She nudged Running Water, who held up the dresses so the Priests could see. "We will go to the top of the Hill and dress our daughters for their wedding, as is the custom among the People."

She felt Running Water's arm quiver with fear and held it tight against her side with her elbow to give them both courage. The young Priest stood without speaking, then turned to his companions, who were whispering and giggling in the grip of their visions. He turned back to the women.

"Well," he said slowly, "I will have a man accompany you. Two Heads," he called over his shoulder, and one of the men stepped forward. "Take these women to the house where the brides are waiting. They have clothing for their daughters who have been chosen."

As Two Heads came closer, Cricket Sings saw with dismay that his face was divided into two halves. One side was smooth and silly with the look of the seeds, but the other was knotted like an evil charm. She lowered her eyes, but kept her face turned in his direction, hoping he would not notice her disgust.

"These grandmothers are going to the top? A little old for brides, aren't they? Tough, you might say."

The third Priest doubled over with laughter. Cricket Sings felt the danger heavy in her belly as she remembered the night flyer. A cold trickle of sweat ran down her ribs.

Two Heads pointed to the dresses. "Perhaps we should see how you old brides look in your fine garments. Put those dresses on, women!" Suddenly, his voice was cruel.

"Do as he says," the herb woman hissed through her teeth to Running Water. They began to put on the dresses. The third Priest came forward and tied a sash around his head, then danced a few wedding steps. All three men began to giggle. Two Heads broke off the gaiety.

"Hurry, I have important business tonight," he said, bowing low and extending an arm toward the stairs leading up into the dark. As the women began to climb, Cricket Sings' heart was pounding so loudly that she feared the young Priest behind them would hear. There was a foul odor in the air and she did not know whether it was the Priests or her own fear she smelled. Running Water stopped to rest for a moment.

"Come on, old woman, hurry along here. I am important and have better things to do."

They began to climb again, puffing and out of breath. Each step was agony to Cricket Sings. At last the top was in sight. The flickering light from a fire reminded her of the last time she had been on top of this hill. A celebration was again in progress and men were dancing. A basket of seeds sat next to the path at the crest of the Hill and Two Heads grabbed a handful, filling his mouth and crunching the seeds between his teeth.

"Here is the house you want," he said, leading the women across a broad meadow toward the far side of the Hill.

As they came closer to the small hut the babbling voices of many young women could be heard above the rhythmic drumming which accompanied the dances. Two Heads left the women outside the hut and ran toward the fire, his duties as escort forgotten. Cricket Sings pulled her sister by the arm toward the door.

"Remember," she spoke under her breath. "They have probably eaten the seeds and will not be the girls you know."

Running Water nodded. Two guards were sprawled at one side of the door, lost in visions. Cricket Sings flipped a mat out of the doorway and stuck her head inside. It was very dark, but she could see the huddled shapes of young women on the floor. Some were lying down and other rested with their backs against the posts which formed the frame of the hut. She turned back to her sister.

"They are far from this World."

"We will find my daughters," answered Running Water. "Perhaps we can reason with them."

The other woman shook her head and entered the hut. She stepped on soft legs and arms, waited for cries of pain, and was startled when giddy laughter rang out instead. The women felt their way carefully to the back wall of the hut where the light glimmered through several holes in the thatch.

"Sister," Running Water whispered from behind. "Here they are, lying together on the floor."

Cricket Sings dropped to her hands and knees and crawled toward the voice. The two girls were curled together so closely that the limbs of one could hardly be separated from those of the other. They were shivering with strange demons. The old woman grasped Running Water's warm hand and pulled her sister's ear close to her mouth.

"We must convince these girls that the Gods sent us, that we are here to take them to their bridegroom."

Running Water squeezed her hand in answer. Together, they began to push and pull the girls to a sitting position. Cricket Sings knelt between them and held each niece close with a comforting arm. She spoke slowly and distinctly.

"We are spirits, disguised as your mother and aunt. We have been sent to take you to the Holy Bridegroom. Be calm, be joyous, this is your destiny. Follow the mother-spirit to join your ancestors."

She felt the fear tense in the young bodies, and rocked until both relaxed against her; then she slipped out of the middle and linked the girls' arms. She whispered once more to her sister.

"We must loosen the thatch at the back of the hut."

Running Water began to crawl over the quivering bodies toward the specks of light which marked the rear wall. The old woman took the hands of her nieces and pulled the girls close.

"We will go to the Gods now. Remember, you must not be frightened. There is no pain in the Holy Way. Glory awaits you."

She pulled the girls to their feet and led them carefully after their mother. Feeling her sister's soft rump in the dark, the old woman stopped abruptly and the girls bumped into her back with murmurs of surprise.

"Shh. You must not tell the others you are first or they will be jealous," she said to calm the whispers. She turned to Running Water. "Have you made an opening?"

"A small hole, feel," Running Water grasped her elbow and the herb woman allowed her arm to be guided to a narrow gap in the thatch.

"We must not take out too much, just push it aside."

Running Water rustled the dry thatch and slipped outside. "I am free," she said.

Cricket Sings tugged on the girls and they stumbled forward. She stepped aside and pushed first one and then the second niece through the opening. Running Water was whispering.

"Hurry, sister, we are close to the edge of the Hill. It will be easy to slide down."

The older woman stuck her head out through the hole. The storm clouds had passed without rain and now the stars were tiny bright eyes in the night.

"I promised Crow Eater we would bring Soon to be Winter. Go to the meeting place and we will follow. Do not wait, but have the men tell Crow Eater where they will camp. He will not leave without his wife."

The girls had begun to moan softly and Running Water grabbed each by a shoulder and shook them.

"Be silent and obey the Gods." She turned back to her sister. "I do not like to leave you alone in this place."

"Nonsense! I am old, but also full of tricks." She paused. "If I do not reach the bottom of the Hill, tell Doe Eyes to keep the bag safe and remember the recipes for Little One."

Running Water's feet made rustling noises in the loose thatching on the ground. Cricket Sings heard a sob.

"Hurry now, the men will be waiting," she said.

The aching in her chest was sharper than any pain she had ever known. Her eyes were wet suddenly and she brushed the back of one hand across her face as the three black shapes disappeared. The hut was crowded and the old woman knelt to search for Soon to be Winter. The dancer might not remember her own name, so the herb woman relied on her sense of touch. She felt the face of each girl in turn, wondering where they had come from. Was this a child she had helped birth? Had this one heard her stories?

Near the doorway, leaning against a post which held up the wall, she found Soon to be Winter. The Seeress did not respond when the old woman touched her. Her spirit had lost its way. Cricket Sings held her face close to the girl's mouth and felt the warm breath on her cheek.

"Sister, little sister, wake up," she whispered as loud as she dared.

There was no spoken answer, but Soon to be Winter moved her legs to a more relaxed position. The old woman sat beside the girl and put an arm around her, pulling her close. She felt the Seeress stiffen and tremble rhythmically several times. It was not a good sign. When the shaking stopped she leaned close to the girl's ear and spoke softly.

"Beautiful dancer, one who knows secret Worlds, wake and answer your sister." The old woman felt the girl's head turn.

"I am so sick, please help me. The visions will not stop," came the slow, whispered answer.

Cricket Sings was stricken with sorrow. The omen of the night flyer was coming true. One of her kind was dying. Who would be the second? The herb woman began to hum and rock, comforting Soon to be Winter as though she were a child. The girl sighed and relaxed. Again the old woman thought of the beautiful, deadly night flyer.

Next to them a woman with a piercing voice shrieked four times and then was silent. Cricket Sings leaned to talk to the screamer.

"Where are the seeds?"

Two more shrieks were again followed by silence.

"I said, where are the seeds?" She made her voice sharp.

"There in the bowl," came the tired answer and the herb woman felt the cold roundness of pottery against her leg. She reached into the opening and touched the tiny seeds. Stirring them with her fingers, she pulled the limp weight of Soon to be Winter closer. The old woman sighed, then closed her hand around the seeds and brought the fist to her mouth. She licked one seed off her fingers, tasting her own sweat, then held her hand tight against her mouth, tipped her head back, and let a few seeds trickle inside, biting them to taste the bitter poison. Her mouth was dry and she chewed and swallowed with difficulty. When her hand was empty, she leaned her head against the pole to wait.

CHAPTER SIXTEEN
Sunrise

The visions began slowly. The hut seemed lighter, as though fire was shining through the walls. Cricket Sings shifted the weight of her friend's body to a more comfortable position against her shoulder. The light did not come from outside the hut. The bodies of the young women had been darker patches in the Night, but now they began to glow. The old woman closed her eyes and pushed hard on the lids with her thumb and fingers until she saw stars. When she opened her eyes the outlines of all the young women in the hut could be seen clearly. The glow was now very bright. She looked up and saw how intricately the thatch of the roof had been woven.

Suddenly the dry marsh grass which formed the thatching began to grow, turning green before her eyes. With the grass came the marsh, the wind ruffling through tall man plants and leaving little ripples dancing across the water. Sun was hot and she loosened her overdress and slipped it off. The wind dried the sweat on her arms. It felt cool and she reached up to loosen her braids, lifting the long hair so the wind could reach her neck. She turned to her lover.

"I will remember this day. I have waited many years."

He laughed and his fine teeth were white in the Sun. "You will have many happy days with me."

He took her comb and began to comb her hair, which was creased from the braids. When the hair lay black and shining across her shoulders he turned and put his head in her lap, closing his eyes against the bright sky.

"So you are happy that I hid behind the tree and played the flute for you?"

"I never knew the music was for me. Only beautiful maidens have lovers; the rest are sold to old men. Our mothers tell us that such husbands are good hunters." She turned and her hair slid along his cheek. "I think a song in the ear is better than a rabbit in the pot."

He sat up suddenly. "How would you know, my plump little wife?" He pinched her arm gently, then flattened his palm on her cheek and looked into her eyes.

She reached up to touch his hand and felt her own wrinkles. The dream World collapsed around her and the thatched roof lowered. Once again she was in the crowded hut. The evil smell was stronger now. She sniffed back her tears and swallowed but the smell remained. Soon to be Winter stirred restlessly, crossing and uncrossing her legs, then muttered a few words. The old woman bent closer.

"What did you say, child?"

"Mmmmh, mmh, where is my husband? I would like to have his babies now, many sons, hunters and stone workers. I am cold, where is the fire?"

"Shhh, now. You have given yourself to the Priests to die as a bride of the Sun King. Do you remember? You were very happy when I met you in the road."

"Cricket Sings, oh sister, I did not know it would be so lonely." The girl began to cry softly, her body jerking with the sobs. "I want to go home to my husband."

"Can you get up? Can you walk?"

Soon to be Winter tried to roll onto her side, but she did not have the strength to balance on her hands and knees. She fell back into the old woman's arms.

"I cannot walk, I cannot dance. Please, I want to go home before the devils come again."

Cricket Sings pulled the young woman close and rocked her, singing a familiar lullaby. She felt the visions coming and turned her head so she could speak into Soon to be Winter's ear.

"I have eaten some of the seeds. It has been many years since I saw my husband Sand Crane. In the same way you long for your husband I wish to see mine. Be still, I will return."

It was fall, the oak leaves hung deep brown from the trees. Leaves of lesser trees hushed and sighed underfoot. Cricket Sings walked on the trail behind Sand Crane, watching his wide shoulders move as he swung his arms. He carried a small pack, his lance, and a bow and arrows. Her medicine bag was heavy on her back, filled with herbs for the winter. She pushed a branch out of the way and felt a movement in the smaller weight at her middle, down where it had begun to swell with the child. She felt the tiny foot kicking.

"Husband!"

He turned and she grabbed his arm in excitement, pulling his hand down flat at the spot where she had felt the movement. His hand was warm and larger than hers. Once again came the soft kicking and she saw his eyes grow round with wonder.

"It is the child?" he asked, dropping his bow and placing both hands on the roundness.

"Yes, the one we made by the river."

He threw back his head and shouted with laughter. It echoed through the woods and a bird screeched in alarm. "So you still remember that time? Well, mother, perhaps we will do better. Come here."

She felt suddenly shy and turned her face down from his frank gaze. "But husband, here on the trail? What if someone is traveling this way?

"Then they will know that I am a lucky man to have a wife who likes lovemaking," he answered and shrugged off his pack. "There is a clearing beyond the big oak tree. We will spread our robe on the leaves." He untied the robe from his pack and led the way.

Cricket Sings followed, her legs trembling with excitement. Sand Crane spread the robe carefully on the leaves and removed his shirt and breechcloth. He turned and smiled, holding out his hand. She put her own hand in his and felt the magic grow between them. She fumbled at her overdress, but the strings at the neck were caught in her braids. Gently her lover pulled at the strings until they were loose. He lifted the overdress up and off. She felt his warm hands on her breasts and pulled at her skirt until she stood naked in the cool air. She pushed out her belly and it grew very round. He laughed.

They knelt on the mat, Sand Crane rubbing and rubbing her belly. She felt so happy that the laughter rose to her mouth and rolled out joyously. Together they worshipped.

As they lay exhausted on the robe afterward she picked up leaves and stuck the stems into his hair. Soon his head bristled with many colors and shapes.

"You look like a tree," she giggled.

He hugged her and the leaves crunched beneath them. She saw the blue sky between the branches before she closed her eyes.

"Cricket Sings," he whispered.

She turned and murmured into his shoulder, nearly asleep.

"Cricket Sings!"

The whisper was louder. She opened her eyes to the darkness of the hut. Her heart fell. She had forgotten the hut, and with it most of her life. A shape was huddled nearby, speaking in a man's voice.

"Cricket Sings, is that you? Please answer!"

She knew the voice. It was Crow Eater, so much like his older brother Sand Crane. "Crow Eater, I am glad you have come." She felt so empty.

"Where is my wife?"

His hand found her arm, then slid down to her hand, which rested on Soon to be Winter's forehead.

"Is this her? Is she alive? Oh, may the Gods bless me and give her back!"

The old woman choked on her tears. The happiest part of her life was gone forever, even the seeds could not help reclaim her lover for more than a few moments. Yet, perhaps the moments were enough.

"We are here," she said in a thick voice. "I have been waiting with your wife. She ate many seeds and has become too weak to walk. I thought perhaps we might crawl out the hole that Running Water left."

"That is the way I came in. We found Running Water and her two girls at the bottom of the Hill. The others have gone to the boat to meet Doe Eyes and the children. They will travel upriver and wait at a place where Wolf Hunter and I killed a deer two summers ago."

"That is good news," the old woman answered slowly. She felt as though she were underwater, with each word coming out of her mouth in a bubble. It took a long time to make the bubbles. "Perhaps we can rouse your wife and she will be strong enough to walk." She sat up a little straighter and shook the girl.

"Soon to be Winter," Crow Eater whispered hoarsely in her ear. "Wife, it is time to go home now."

There was no answer. Cricket Sings felt the body of her friend begin to tremble again. The shuddering seemed to start at the girl's feet, moved up her body in waves, then stopped as suddenly as it had begun.

"She is very sick. There are no cures for the seeds, you know. Some need very few to see the visions and if they eat more their bodies become detached from the soul. This has happened to your wife."

"Will she get better?" Crow Eater's voice was hoarse with fear. "I think she will die."

There was a long silence. Cricket Sings felt arrows of pain flying up and down her back. She had been sitting in one position for a long time. Pushing Crow Eater back with one hand, she lifted the young woman's head into his arms.

"Sit here beside me." Words were very difficult for her now. She wanted to run away to the spirit World where Sand Crane was waiting. She could feel him, impatient ahead on the trail. She remembered how his eyes flashed when he smiled.

Crow Eater sat crosslegged in front of her with his wife's head on his lap. Cricket Sings could see clearly as he brushed the matted hair back from the once-beautiful face and bent over her. He was crying, his shoulders shaking silently.

"She is all I have, she is my life." His voice was heavy with tears.

"I think you should go. She will never be well enough to travel. I think she may die very soon now. I will stay here with her. Such events have been foretold by certain signs. Remember, your wife chose to die for the Sun King. She wanted you to be proud." Cricket Sings' voice was very low now. She was so tired and the seeds were humming in her skull.

Crow Eater bent over his wife once more. He whispered her name but there was no answer. He turned his face up to the old woman, his eyes searching blindly in the dark for her expression.

"It will always be winter without her." He choked on the words.

"I know, it was that way for me without Sand Crane. After he died I did not want to live. But one day you will see that Sun is shining and the birds are flying low. I will take good care of Soon to be Winter. Go now, and watch the Sunrise for her." She reached out and pushed against his chest with her palm, then lifted Soon to be Winter's shoulders onto her lap once again.

Crow Eater stood slowly, wiping his eyes. His hands fell to his sides and his shoulders slumped. "What will I tell the others?"

"Tell them to remember the stories."

"I will not forget."

"Go, go now, before the guards check."

He bent and smoothed Soon to be Winter's fine hair back from her forehead once more, then laid his cheek against hers for a moment. He whispered, but the old woman could not hear what he said.

"May the Sun shine, old woman," he said as he stood.

She did not turn her head to watch him go. There was a rustling at the back of the hut and then she was alone with the brides once more. Even the screamer was quiet. The drums of the Priests continued. Her head was aching and it began to throb in rhythm with the drumming. She wanted Sand Crane, but now she could not feel his spirit. The evil smell was very strong.

When the vision came she was a small child, and the Priest who stood over her wore an angry mask. She knew he was a Priest and had come to heal her, but still she was afraid. The mask was painted in red and black lines with staring eyes and bushy hair, ugly enough to frighten any spirit.

Her broken leg was throbbing, and she tried to ease the pain by moving. A jolt of agony shot up past her knee and into her belly. She turned her face into the soft furred deerskin so the Priest could not see the hot tears. She knew dying would be easier than this pain.

The Priest was shaking her now and pain ran through her like a river as he tried to drive out the evil.

"Old woman, old woman, wake up I say!"

She looked up into the smooth wide-eyed face of a young Priest. The mask and the pain had been a part of her visions.

"What are you doing here?" the Priest asked impatiently.

She saw that he was one of the young servants of the former Eagle. "I am here to help my friend, Soon to be Winter. She gave herself as a bride for the Sun King, but has eaten too many seeds.

I think she will die soon." She reached down and felt Soon to be Winter's chest rising and falling unevenly.

The young man's eyes were very big from the seeds. "Will you die for the Sun?" he asked.

She thought for a moment about the spirit world where Sand Crane waited eagerly. "It is time," she said, her voice rich with dignity.

Three other Priests entered the hut and began to prod and push the weak young women to get them to stand.

"Hurry, hurry, the Sun will be rising," one said.

With groans and shrieks the brides clambered to their feet. Cricket Sings realized that light was now coming from outside the hut. It was nearly dawn.

"Help me with this one," she said.

She picked up Soon to be Winter's arm and handed it to the Priest. He pulled. The girl was limp and her head swung back from her neck, the long hair partially unbraided. Her eyes were sunken and the breath whistled through her nostrils. The Priest pulled harder and put his arm around the girl, lifting her to her feet. The Seeress's legs were limp, as though she were already dead. Groaning, Cricket Sings stood. Her whole body was stiff and aching. The old woman put her arm around Soon to be Winter and together she and the Priest dragged the girl toward the door of the hut.

Outside the air was cool and grey with the smoke of many fires. Sun was glowing below the horizon, but the City was silent. Even the drums of the Priests had ceased to beat. Only a few birds had begun their morning songs. At the east edge of the mound the faithful were gathered to send the spirit of the Sun King on its long flight. The body was wrapped in fine robes, Cricket Sings could see the dark fur tied with woven ropes. Moon huddled at the dead man's feet, hunched in grief, her head covered by a cloak. She, too, would join her husband in the spirit World this morning.

The Eagle, now the new Sun King, stood at his father's head. He wore the yellow cloak of finest feathers and a wooden mask hid his face. The youth had become a God.

Cricket Sings stumbled on a flute lying beside the path. She stopped and the young Priest made an annoyed click with his tongue. She bent and picked up the flute, noting the smooth wood from which it was made, then curved her hand around it and rose to her full height.

The maidens were being pushed to their knees in a row behind the funeral bier. Some wavered and one fell onto her side, but no one made a sound. The Priest pulled at Soon to be Winter's arm and the old woman followed. When they were even with the line the Priest dropped the Seeress and Cricket Sings felt the body slide down onto the ground. She tried to pull the girl's head against her, but then gave up and arranged her friend comfortably on the ground.

The evil smell was overpowering. The Sun King picked up a black bowl which had been sitting near his father's head. He went to the north end of the line where the first maidens had gathered. The old woman was at the south end and strained to see what he was doing. He offered the bowl to the first maiden, who sipped and sat back on her heels. In a few moments she fell onto her side and two Priests picked up her body and laid it next to the dead man. The Sun King went down the line. Each girl drank in turn from the bowl and in turn died. When he came to the young woman who had fallen to the ground, the man bent and helped her to a sitting position so she might drink. Soon to be Winter was next. Cricket Sings looked carefully at the Sun King. She could not see his eyes behind the slits in the mask. It was painted in red and black stripes like the mask of her childhood. He was looking at her and the mask nodded once.

"The spirit has flown from her body," the old woman said. "Put the potion in her mouth, but she will die even without poison."

The Sun King nodded again silently and bent over the Seeress. Soon to be Winter was no longer beautiful. The grey marks of death were on her face. He pushed down on her chin with a careful finger and tilted the bowl so that the sticky liquid ran into her mouth and down her cheek. The breath gurgled in Soon to be Winter's throat for a moment and then she was silent.

Now the Sun King stood before Cricket Sings. She looked hard at the eye slits.

"I need a favor," she said boldly.

"Such was my promise," came the calm, deep answer.

The old woman felt relief flowing through her chest. She took a deep breath. "When I am dead, put my bones in the earth with my ancestors so my spirit will find a place to rest."

"It will be done." He offered the poison.

She took the bowl. It was surprisingly heavy and she nearly dropped it. Raising the bowl to her lips, the old woman drank. The liquid was bitter and sour at once, so thick that sickness rose in her throat. She swallowed, then swallowed again. Blackness grew in her belly, but she felt her spirit soar.

Cricket Sings woke with a jerk. She heard the soft breathing of her husband and saw the coals of their fire glowing outside the doorway. Beside her Sand Crane turned in his sleep and smacked his lips. She rolled close to him and put her cheek against his moist shoulder, her arm around his chest. She licked the skin and tasted his sweat.

"I had a strange dream," she said.

"Hmmm?" he murmured.

"I said, I dreamed I was old."

"Even when your children are grown you will not be old." His voice was muffled in the fur robes.

She pushed her belly tight against him. The roundness of the new one fit into the warm hollow of his lower back. He sighed and spoke.

"Go to sleep, woman."

She slept.

Suggestions For Further Reading

Adams, William R. "Archaeozoological Studies at Cahokia." Xeroxed. Ann Arbor: University of Michigan, Museum of Anthropology. N.D.

Baker, Frank C. "Additional Notes on Animal Life Associated with the Mound Builders of Illinois," *Transactions of the Illinois State Academy of Science,* Vol 23: 231–35 (1931).

—————. "A Study in Ethnozoology of the Prehistoric Indians of Illinois," *Transactions of the American Philosophical Society,* **32:** 51–77, (1941).

—————. "The Use of Molluscan Shells by the Cahokia Mound Builders," *Transactions of the Illinois State Academy of Science,* **16:** 328–34 (1923).

—————. "The Use of Animal Life by the Mound Building Indians of Illinois," *Transactions of the Illinois State Academy of Science,* **22:** 41–64 (1930).

Baldwin, Gordon C. *Games of the American Indian.* New York: Grosset and Dunlap, Inc., 1969.

Bandelier, Adolf F. *The Delight Makers.* New York: Harcourt Brace Jovanovich, Inc., 1971.

Barrett, Samuel A. "Ancient Aztalan," *Bulletin of the Public Museum* of the City of Milwaukee, Vol. 13 (1933).

Beckwith, Hiram Williams. *The Illinois and Indiana Indians.* New York: Arno Press, 1975.

Bleed, Peter. "Notes on Aztalan Shell-tempered Pottery," *The Wisconsin Archaeologist,* **51**(1), N.S.: 1–20 (1970).

Brandt, Keith. "American Bottoms Settlements," pp. 63–69, in M.L. Fowler (ed.), *The University of Wisconsin-Milwaukee Cahokia Archaeology Project.* Milwaukee: The University of Wisconsin-Milwaukee, 1972.

Burt, William Henry. *Mammals of the Great Lakes Region.* Ann Arbor: University of Michigan Press, 1957.

Carr, Archie. *Handbook of Turtles.* Ithaca, N.Y.: Cornell University Press, 1952.

Chmurny, William W. "The Ecology of the Middle Mississippian Occupation of the American Bottom." Unpublished Ph.D. Dissertation, University of Illinois, 1973.

Cole, Fay-Cooper, *et al. Kincaid: A Prehistoric Illinois Metropolis.* Chicago: University of Chicago Press, 1951.

Compton, Margaret. *American Indian Fairy Tales.* New York: Dodd, Mead and Company, 1971.

Conant, A. J. *Footprints of Vanished Races in the Mississippi Valley.* St. Louis: Chancy R. Barns, 1879.

Cory, Charles B. *The Birds of Illinois and Wisconsin.* Chicago, Illinois: Field Museum of Natural History, Publication 131. Zoological Series Volume 9 (1909).

Crook, A. R. *The Origin of the Cahokia Mounds.* Springfield, Ill.: Bulletin of the Illinois State Museum, 1922.

Curtis, Edward S. *Portraits from North American Indian Life.* U.S.A.: Outerbridge and Lazard, Inc., 1972.

Denny, Sidney G. *The Archaeology of the Big Muddy River Basin of Southern Illinois.* Unpublished Ph.D. Dissertation, Southern Illinois University, 1972. 262 pp.

Deuel, Thorne. *American Indian Ways of Life.* Springfield, Ill.: The Illinois State Museum, 1968.

————————. *Illinois Records of 1000 A.D.* Springfield, Ill.: Illinois State Museum, 1948.

————————. *Power Adaptations and Changing Cultures.* Springfield, Illinois: Illinois State Museum, 1976.

Elder, William H. "Primeval Deer Hunting Pressures Revealed by Remains From American Indian Middens," *Journal of Wildlife Management,* 29:366–70.

Fowler, Melvin L. "Agriculture and Village Settlement in the North American East: The Central Mississippi Valley Area, A Case History." *XXXVI Congreso Internacional de Americanistas,* Vol. 1, pp. 229–40.

———————— (ed.). "American Bottoms Archaeology, July 1, 1961–June 30, 1962," *Illinois Archaeological Survey, First Annual Report.* Urbana, Ill.: University of Illinois, 1962.

—————. *American Bottoms Archaeology: Second Annual Report, July 1, 1962 to June 30, 1963.* Urbana, Ill.: Illinois Archeological Survey, 1963.

—————, and Robert L. Hall. *Archaeological Phases at Cahokia.* Springfield, Ill.: Illinois State Museum, 1972.

—————. *Cahokia: Ancient Capital of the Midwest.* Addison–Wesley Module in Anthropology, No. 48. Reading, Mass.: Addison–Wesley Publishing Co., Inc., 1974.

————— (ed.). *Cahokia Archaeology: Field Reports.* Papers in Anthropology, No. 3. Springfield, Ill.: Illinois State Museum, 1975.

————— (ed.). *Explorations in Cahokia Archaeology.* Illinois Archaeological Survey, Bulletin No. 7. Urbana, Ill.: University of Illinois, 1977.

—————. "Middle Mississippian Agricultural Fields," *American Antiquity,* **34:** 365–75.

Gregg, Michael. "Biological Resource Base and Area Ecology." In M.L. Fowler (ed.), *The University of Wisconsin-Milwaukee Cahokia Archaeology Project,* pp. 41–45. Mimeographed.

Griffin, James B. "The Cahokia Ceramic Complexes." *Proceedings of the 5th Plains Conference,* John L. Champe (ed.). University of Nebraska Laboratory of Anthropology, Notebook No. 1, pp. 44–57.

Hardoy, Jorge E. *Pre-Columbian Cities.* New York: Walker and Company, 1974.

Harn, Alan D. *The Prehistory of Dickson Mounds: A Preliminary Report.* Springfield, Ill.: The Illinois State Museum, 1971.

Heiser, Charles B. "The Origin and Development of the Cultivated Sunflower," *The American Biology Teacher,* **17:** 161–167.

—————. "The Sunflower Among the North American Indians," *Proceedings of the American Philosophical Society,* **95:** 432–88 (1951).

Hoffmeiter, Donald F., and Carl O. Mohr. *Fieldbook of Illinois Mammals.* Springfield, Ill.: Illinois Natural History Survey, Manual 4.

Hungry Wolf, Adolf. *Good Medicine in Glacier National Park.* Golden, B.C.: Good Medicine Books, 1971.

Hurlbert, Archer B. *Paths of the Mound-Building Indians and Great Game Animals.* Historic Highways of America, Vol. 1. New York: AMS Press, 1971. Original series published 1902–1905.

Illinois Archaeological Survey, Inc. *Mississippian Site Archaeology in Illinois.* Urbana, Ill.: University of Illinois, 1975. Bulletin No. 8.

—————. *Perspectives in Cahokia Archaeology.* Urbana, Ill.: University of Illinois, 1975. Bulletin No. 10.

Iseminger, William R. "Cahokia, A Mississippian Metropolis." *Historic Illinois,* **2(6):** 1–4 (April 1980.) Publication of Illinois Department of Conservation, Division of Historic Sites.

Jennings, Jesse D., and Edward Norbeck (eds.). *Prehistoric Man in the New World.* Chicago: University of Chicago Press, 1964.

Johnston, Alexander. *"Chenopodium album* as a Food Plant in Blackfoot Indian Prehistory." *Ecology,* **43**: 129–30.

Jones, Louis Thomas. *Love–Indian Style.* San Antonio, Texas: The Naylor Company, 1973.

Josephy, Alvin M., Jr. *The Indian Heritage of America.* New York: Bantam Books, 1968.

Kaplan, Lawrence. "Archaeology and Domestication in American *Phaseolus* (beans)." *Economic Botany* **19**: 358–68.

Krupp, E.C. "Cahokia, Corn, Commerce and the Cosmos." *Griffith Observer,* **41(5)**: 10–23 (May 1977).

Lewis, Meriwether. *The Lewis and Clark Expedition.* Philadelphia and New York: J.B. Lippincott Company, 1961.

Marriott, Alice, and Carol K. Rachlin. *American Indian Mythology.* New York: Thomas Y. Crowell Company, 1968.

Maurer, Evan M. *The Native American Heritage, A Survey of North American Art.* Chicago: The Art Institute of Chicago, 1977.

Morse, Dan. *Ancient Disease in the Midwest.* Springfield, Ill.: The Illinois State Museum, 1978.

O'Brien, Patricia J. "Urbanism, Cahokia and Middle Mississippian." *Archaeology,* **25(3)**: 189–97 (June 1972).

Ortiz de Montellano, Bernard R. "Aztec Cannibalism: An Ecological Necessity?" *Science,* **200:(4342)**: 611–17 (12 May 1978).

Parmalee, Paul W. "Animal Remains from the Aztalan Site, Jefferson County, Wisconsin." *The Wisconsin Archaeologist,* **41**: 1–10.

_____. "Use of Mammalian Skulls and Mandibles by Prehistoric Indians of Illinois," *Transactions of the Illinois State Academy of Science,* **52**: 85–95.

Perino, Gregory. "Cahokia." *Central States Archaeological Journal,* **3(3)**: 84–88 (1957).

_____. "Recent Information from Cahokia and Its Satellites." *Central States Archaeological Journal,* **6(4)**: 130–38 (1959).

Pfeiffer, John. "America's First City." *Horizon,* **16(2)**: 58–63 (Spring 1974).

Quimby, George I. "A Year with a Chippewa Family 1763-1764." *Ethnohistory,* **9**: 217–39.

Ridgway, Robert. *The Ornithology of Illinois,* Volume I: *Descriptive Catalog.* Springfield: Natural History Survey of Illinois, 1889

Roper, Donna C. *The Distribution of Middle Woodland Sites Within the Environment of the Lower Sangamon River, Illinois.* Springfield, Ill.: Illinois State Museum, 1974.

Silverberg, Robert. *Mound Builders of Ancient America.* Greenwich, Conn.: New York Graphic Society Ltd., 1968.

Stone, Eric. *Medicine Among the American Indians.* New York: Hafner Publishing Company, 1962.

Streuver, Stuart, and Felicia Antonelli Holton. *Koster: Americans in Search of Their Prehistoric Past.* Garden City, N.Y.: Anchor Press/Doubleday, 1979.

Streuver, Stuart. *Prehistoric Agriculture.* Garden City, N.Y.: Natural History Press, 1971.

Stuart, George E. "Who Were the Mound Builders?" *National Geographic,* **142(6):** 782–801 (December 1972).

Temple, Wayne C. *Indian Villages of the Illinois Country.* Springfield, Ill.: The Illinois State Museum, 1966.

Titterington, P.F. *The Cahokia Mound Group and Its Village Site Materials.* Cahokia, Ill.: Cahokia Mounds Museum Society, 1977. Originally published in 1938.

Van der Schalie, Henry. "The Mussels of the Mississippi River." *American Midland Naturalist,* **44:** 448–66.

Waselkov, G. "Prehistoric Agriculture in the Central Mississippi Valley." *Agricultural History,* **51:** 513–19 (July 1977).

Wilford, Lloyd A., Elden Johnson and Joan Vicinius. *Burial Mounds of Central Minnesota.* St. Paul, Minn., Historical Society, 1969.

Wilford, Lloyd A. *Burial Mounds of the Red River Headwaters.* St. Paul, Minn.: Minnesota Historical Society, 1970.

Willey, Gordon R. "The Prehistoric Civilizations of Nuclear America," *American Anthropologist,* **57:** 571–93.

Wissler, Clark. *The Relation of Nature to Man in Aboriginal America.* New York: AMS Press, 1971.

Wittry, Warren L. "An American Woodhenge," *Cranbrook Institute of Science Newsletter,* **33(9):** 102–7.